The Naked Ballerina

A.K. HIRSCH

COVER ART BY
JEWEL MCDANIELS

ContentRising LLC Publishing

Published by ContentRising LLC, February 2016
www.contentrising.com
contact@contentrising.com

ISBN 13: 978-0-692-64015-9
ISBN: 0-692-64015-0

To the city of Los Angeles

PROLOGUE

At least it was a classic spot, right next to the Hyperion Bridge, which spans the trickling Los Angeles River near the border of Los Feliz and Glendale. Almost 5 p.m. and the light was fading. Why not do it at high noon? No, definitely pick a time when everyone's vision would be at the mercy of the descending darkness. Genius.

I wound down the window to wake myself up a bit as I negotiated some traffic headed east on Los Feliz Boulevard. A whoosh of warm air flooded in and caressed the cabin of my tragic, plastic-encrusted rental car. I'd never use my own ride for a crazy job like this, I actually care about her. As I started wondering who would actually buy such a domestic shitbox other than a rental agency, I got a text notification on my phone. Carefully checking my mirrors for cops, I quickly glanced at the screen: "We are ON. OK?" Fine. I responded in the affirmative and engaged the pitiful passing gear to kick the car past a slow moving brown van in front of me. Had brown ever been a good choice? Focus, Marsden...

The location was right on the other side of the river. I pulled off into the parking lot. It turned out to be an abandoned miniature golf course. What a pleasant place for a shady internet deal. Off to one side of the driveway there was a six foot tall fiberglass clown welcoming non-existent customers with one busted eye. I guessed the eyes had been cheerfully lit up at some point. Not anymore. It was pretty depressing. A very fitting place for my latest job.

Before I had a chance to start feeling too sorry for myself, I spied my "client." Julius Forsythe stood next to a mirror-black 1972 Cadillac Eldorado. Pristine condition, just as he'd described. To be fair, though the car wasn't my particular cup of tea, I could see why everyone was going to such lengths. Four grand over asking is never something for a seller to pass up, though it screams "to good to be true" at you with an industrial bullhorn.

As I stepped out of my car: "Mr. Marsden! Good to see you again. What'd I tell you, perfect! Just perfect." He gestured like a TV host revealing a fabulous prize.

"I'll give you that, it is gorgeous. You could sell it to anyone. Why the extra drama?"

He went from grin to grimace instantaneously.

"Just got to get rid of it, you know? And he offered me way over asking, so why not?"

Julius had a modern-looking version of a comb-over that anyone could see was terrible. Every now and again he would snag a black plastic comb out of his back pocket and slide it through the wispy hairs a few times. He wore a tattered polo shirt and slacks that appeared to only be about thirty years old, give or take. The shirt could barely contain the pot belly that seemed just barely attached to his gangly frame. Speaking of frames, his glasses all seemed to be sunglasses. When he first showed up at my office, he was wearing a similar outfit, but different glasses. Boy was I scraping the bottom of the barrel these days.

The guy had hired me as some muscle for a car sale he set up on one of those very popular online classified sites. I'd accompany him for the deal, make sure all was copasetic and ensure he got his $15,000 to the bank without incident, then chauffeur him back to his place in Hollywood. This was not the kind of job a private detective should have to take. But the world seemed to be headed in a dire direction lately; between the recession and the ill-informed notion that the internet has all the answers for free, modern times are challenging for PIs. Because the real world is not in fact free, it's hard to turn down $500 for one day's work.

Of course the generous fee also radiated red flags; it was simply too much money for the supposedly simple task of overseeing a used car transaction, but maybe this was the new normal people were always talking about. Either way, I figured I had to take the gig.

"I'm going to call them alright? I'm using speaker, so you can hear the details, to make sure it all sounds good." He took his phone out of his pants pocket and laid it carefully on the hood of the Caddy.

I was flattered he thought I could analyze such details from a scratchy cellphone call, but his misplaced faith only served to make me doubt Julius even more. I had been under the impression he was expecting the deal, with a man known only as "Santa," to go down smooth. Back in the office he had tried to tell me Santa was a nickname for an old, trustworthy acquaintance. I always doubt when people say such things, but I hadn't bothered to look into it, mostly because I didn't want to talk myself out of a job. He dialed and Santa picked up on the first ring.

"Heloo? This is Julius, yeah?"

"Yup, Julius here. We're here and waiting." He beamed at me. I was unimpressed and made sure he saw it.

"Alright man, we'll be there in, like, a minute. But, um, who's we, man?"

"Oh just a friend, you know, someone has to drive me back, not like I expected you guys to!" He forced a shrill laugh that threatened to break the windshield of his prized vehicle.

I remained silent as a few more minutes ticked off the clock and the sun fell a few inches further behind the hills. I desperately wanted to be indignant, but remembered my money was not linked to time. So I took a seat on my own hood and observed Julius nervously try to smoke a ciga-rette while we waited.

Finally, Santa and company arrived in a charcoal-colored SUV. They pulled up and three rough-looking gentlemen jumped out, followed by a fourth, who I guessed to be Santa himself. Of course he was shorter than his companions. And about a thousand times grittier. I had really been hoping the buyers would be a standup group that just wanted to do business. Then again, it hadn't really been my year.

Julius moved in to welcome Santa, but was quickly shut down by the men who'd jumped out with their apparent boss. They gently pushed Julius back. Without speaking, Santa circumnavigated the Caddy and seemed to like what he saw. He didn't smile, but he did pull out an envelope and held it out to Julius.

My client took the envelope, but Santa didn't let it go without a little hesitation. Something about that didn't sit well.

I braced for a faux pas from Julius, and had a quick flashback to when I'd offered to carry a piece for the mission. It cost extra, and no one had asked me to do it before, but I made it a point to always put it on the table, to make sure everyone felt well-serviced. He'd said it wasn't that kind of deal, so no way we'd need it. I'd decided to take him at his word, since the mere presence of guns always seems to escalate things anyway.

To my relief, Julius took the envelope without so much as a whimper. He simply bowed a little, handed the key to Santa and walked over to the passenger side of my car; he motioned for me to take my position as driver. Meanwhile, one of Santa's guys got into the Caddy and quickly slid out of the parking lot.

When I looked over at Julius, he was counting the money. I thought I'd hear some complaints or jubilation, but he just looked relieved. That's when I looked up and saw Santa on the phone in the front passenger seat of the SUV. He was nodding and then he grinned at us and the money a little too widely. This was exactly the kind of deal the news warns you about with these kinds of classified sites. Julius was about to get screwed, and so was I.

Julius and I probably could have had at least half an argument before we would've been killed, but I decided to short-circuit the process. Without saying anything, I grabbed the shifter behind the steering wheel, jammed it into drive and peeled out. I saw Santa's sunglasses fall down his nose as he flashed a silver pistol and yelled in his driver's ear.

I plunged back across the bridge and swung right. Part of me thought there was no way someone was actually going to chase us; ripping someone off is risky and usually takes some extra energy on the part of a would-be villain. At first common sense seemed to win the day. After my dramatic driving I checked the rearview and realized there appeared to be no pursuers, so I calmly pulled up at the light to make a left back onto Los Feliz Boulevard. I looked over and smiled a little at Julius, who grinned dumbly back. That's as far as the bonding got though, as our little rental was violently punted out into the middle of the intersection, the back window shattering from the impact. The mirror revealed the SUV had in fact followed us, probably using a side street, and was approaching very rapidly with the intent to ram again. Now the $500 was looking downright trivial. I made a mental note to rework my pricing scheme.

Without hesitation I gunned it through the intersection, and screeched hard to the left, back toward Hollywood. I didn't really have a destination in mind, but I figured knowing the territory could at least level the playing field, if not yield some advantage. The idea sounded professional enough at least.

I accelerated past ninety and quickly found myself at the limit of the shuddering sub-compact's cruelly pathetic performance. The SUV was behind us and gaining. I took the turn onto Western fast and felt pretty good about it. The more unwieldy SUV would definitely have to slow down, but I still needed a plan. I looked to Julius, who could only contribute a fantastic impression of a very pale corpse. Another wide turn without stopping for the light, and we found ourselves on Hollywood Boulevard. I took a moment to marvel at the number of signals I had just run without so much as a hint of police interference.

Then a bullet took the rearview completely off. Severed it. That got my attention, and I finally started to sweat in earnest. I'd actually been shot at, or at least near, on a job before, but I hadn't really felt any malice behind it. This time the bullets seemed serious.

The SUV was maybe three car lengths back. There was no end game to this chase. I only saw gore and lead in my future.

A police cruiser was parked on the right side of the street about three blocks up. Their light bar was on, and a very lonely-looking hatchback was just pulling back into traffic after being taught a lesson. Thank God for the LAPD. I took aim and rammed the cruiser from behind at about forty miles per hour.

Airbags deployed. Teeth ground. Sweat flew. We came to a pretty fast halt, which was immediately interrupted by the SUV plowing into the back of our already crumpled rental. Metal crunched and shredded as the three car pile-up came to a stop in the middle of Hollywood Boulevard.

Officers jumped out, dazed but weapons drawn. I'd seen what was coming, but apparently the trembling Julius had only figured it out after the fact. He looked like he was struggling to grasp our sudden lack of motion. I immediately threw my empty hands out the window.

Then, something familiar, a crusty voice: "Jesus Christ, Duncan Marsden? Is that you? Shit!" Officer Dowell lowered his gun just a tick as he made the identification. Finally, a tiny crumb of luck.

My Hollywood lifestyle does yield rewards at times. I'd had many a whiskey with the now slightly shaken Officer Dowell, a self-styled protégé of my friend, investigator Quinlin Halle of the district attorney's office. He'd always coveted Quin's position and had been gunning for it, at least in his mind, for about three years, despite his glaring lack of any kind of investigatory experience.

Before I'd gotten my head right and picked the pieces of safety glass out of my hair, Quinlin had been contacted, and Santa and company handcuffed.

Such was my life before she called…

PART I

The Pornographer

1

A little after 1 p.m. on a Monday burdened by an unusually oppressive grey ceiling of clouds, I walked over to the ghostly entrance of the Valiant Ballet Company. Theaters and the like always look ghostly in the day, and I was never too big a fan of them at night either, but it was where the woman on the phone had wanted to meet, so there I was.

I tried to peer through the old smoky glass to assess if anyone was there, or if this was just another waste of time in a day full of wasted time. Not seeing any movement, I rapped on the door three times with my knuckles and waited. I noticed the door was not only locked, but chained shut on the inside. I didn't have time to notice anything else, because I looked up to find a shape materializing out of the soupy blackness that filled the theater's lobby.

The man was reminiscent of a stick insect; he was all narrow lines and bulging eyes. An older insect to be sure, with silvery, stringy hair, and a sagging, wistful visage. He pulled up short on the other side of the doors and started rummaging through his coveralls, not giving me more than a corner of his eye. I didn't know people still wore coveralls.

After a time he decided he had found the right key, moseyed on closer to the doors and started the unlocking procedure. He seemed not to care that I was sizing him up. Finally, with the doors unlocked and the chains removed, he opened the door inward for me. I started:

"Thanks. I'm Duncan here to see…a Ms. Marie Costello."

He looked at me for the first time in earnest. I saw some gears working, then he grunted:

"Mrs."

With that he turned and beckoned me to follow him through the deserted lobby. I followed.

He led me through the stuffy malaise toward the only light, which was seeping from an anteroom off the main lobby. As I reached the haloed door, I turned just in time to watch the thin bug disappear back into the gloom.

The anteroom proved to be a small office, apparently used by the head of the company, or so I assumed. It was spartan, containing only a barren desk and a couple of chairs for furniture, a computer and a small half-dead potted plant in the corner. It wasn't shocking the plant was dying, as there were no windows.

Something else did catch my eye though. A statuesque and richly porcelained woman of about twenty-seven sat on the desk smoking a long, filterless cigarette that hadn't been in fashion for approximately half a century. Having said that, I only glanced at the cigarette, as my eyes were more urgently drawn to her impressive set of legs. There were two, and they were crossed in the most elegant way, as though she had put some thought into it. Her short pleated skirt only served to emphasize those particular assets. I caught myself and decided to go to work:

"Are you Ms. Marie Costello?"

"-Mrs. I assume you're Duncan Marsden."

"I am." I carefully took a business card that read "Duncan Marsden, Private Investigator," and listed my email and cellphone number, out of my wallet and handed it in her general direction. She plucked it from my grasp, looked at it and twisted it in her hands as if to validate its legitimacy. She giggled under a cloud of very chic cigarette smoke.

"I didn't know you people actually still existed."

"Well I guess you took a risk then, calling me."

She took another deep drag and looked me up and down like a slab of meat. I didn't mind.

"Alright, well, I guess I'll get right to it," she said.

She hopped off the front of the desk carefully and swaggered back to the other side. It was a very deliberate saunter so I made sure to watch closely. She finished the show and sat down in the leatherette executive chair behind the archaic desk. There was a noticeable tear in the material just past her right ear. It was at that point that I saw the lonely plaque on the desktop that read: Edmond Costello, Dir.

"So this isn't *your* desk."

"It is for now. Is there a problem?"

"Of course not, I'm sure Edmond doesn't mind."

She batted her long lashes enough to blow out all the candles on a birthday cake and pursed her seemingly permanently puckered lips.

"He lets me use it for my business too."

"This is only *your* business?"

"You certainly get right to it, considering I haven't even told you why I need a detective yet."

"Private detective."

"Of course," she said quickly.

She took another puff on her cigarette and dashed the rest carelessly in a shabby faux amber ashtray.

"Well I'm not really sure how to approach this, so I guess I'll just come out and say it."

"That's usually best."

Before I could embellish my response we were pounced upon by the unfortunate Mr. to her Mrs. The man who now appeared in the doorway was about what I had expected, minus the grace and fitness of those normally associated with the world of dance. He was about my height, with dark brown hair and beadier eyes than a man normally deserves. The slight pudginess around his midsection didn't look like it belonged on his otherwise lithe frame, but there it was, refusing to make itself discreet. He was handsome about seven years ago, maybe ten. His brow glistened a tiny bit as he sussed up the situation. I couldn't figure out who was really the dominant force in the room, her or him; but the balance was shifting so fluidly it'd be stupid to assume it was the man, just because he was a him.

"I didn't know you people really still existed," he said carelessly.

"That seems to be a popular sentiment around here."

I obviously used a word that was just slightly too large, as he paused and looked doubtfully toward Mrs. Costello.

"Well it was her idea." He nodded toward his clearly better half. "I think it's just a complete waste of time. Couldn't she just use the internet for this?"

I responded carefully: "Well maybe it's a waste of time. But if she wanted to use the internet for a mediocre pseudo-investigation, I assume I wouldn't be here, Mr.-"

"Edmond Costello." He gave me the severe look of a shark eyeing a school of pathetic, tiny fish.

"So tell me Mr..."

"Marsden. Duncan Marsden."

"So tell me Mr. Marsden, are you regulated by the state to protect our privacy?"

"Oh, you're hiring me too?"

The statue spoke up: "Only I did," she said.

His brow began to furrow and a suspicious look crept from his forehead to his mouth.

I replied, cautiously: "I'm regulated by the state it's true, but not to protect your privacy, that's a matter of my way of doing business, and I take it very seriously. Her privacy, as my client, that is."

That seemed to simultaneously quiet him and prime him for combat. He took a step in my direction and seemed to draw in a subtle breath. Before he could take what I gauged would be a probably feeble swing, she interrupted:

"I need you to follow my younger sister Stacy. Is that something you can do?"

"I can. Why would you want me to do a thing like that?"

"That sounds pretty accusatory coming from you."

"I just like to operate with as many facts as possible before getting dirty. I try to be ethical."

The man in the corner just guffawed and checked his cell phone.

She continued: "I think she's being taken advantage of."

The unfortunate man made for the door: "Not worth it, hon." With that he turned, exited the room and faded back into the gloom of the lobby.

Her husband's departure perked me up and I picked up where she left off: "How so?"

She paused a second, took out another cigarette, and lit it with a small, red disposable lighter as she opened a desk drawer. She produced what appeared to be a photograph, of which she only delicately touched the borders, as if she might bruise the subject. She handed it across the scarred desk.

It was a real picture alright, printed on real photograph-ic paper, like in the old days. This picture, however, was not your run of the mill color photo. It depicted a young, slender, pale girl or perhaps woman, sitting rigidly on the edge of a pool. She wasn't wearing anything. After what I felt was an appropriate amount of time, I looked up to find Mrs. Costello's deep, ocean blue eyes staring right at me.

"I found this when I was over at her apartment," she said quietly.

"So?"

"I think she's being exploited."

"How old is she?" I asked in my expressly professional tone.

"She just turned nineteen."

"Well, it's legal."

"She is now."

What's her full name?

"Do you really need that just to follow a person?"

I shifted my eyebrows as if analyzing the photo more closely, and, against my better judgement, moved on.

"You think she's being forced to take these photos? Blackmailed?"

"That's what I'd like to know. I guess young people are known to make questionable decisions. Maybe this was hers, but it doesn't fit her character in my opinion."

She took another drag of her second cigarette and stared at me expectantly. For many this biased logic would have warranted at least a cursory challenge. I decided quickly that there were worse jobs out there, and opted not to say a word.

"Alright."

"What's your rate, just to confirm?"

"Why not go to the police with this?"

"The company doesn't need it; I don't need it… dance takes a lot of focus Mr. Marsden."

She playfully traced something invisible on the table-top with a delicate finger and looked up again.

I offered: "My rate is two hundred dollars a day plus expenses."

She took a deep breath, this time of relatively clean, smoke-free Los Angeles air.

"Alright, so you'll do it?"

"Do you have a starting point for me?"

She tenderly flipped over the photo and wrote down what appeared to be an address.

"Here's her address. Tail her from there. She goes somewhere a few nights a week seems like, but won't tell me where."

"Thanks for your advice, but yes, I'll figure out where she goes."

"She's a night owl and, well, is pretty uninhibited… but not like in the photo."

"Drugs?"

A hesitant nod was all she could muster.

"How would you like me to report?"

She took a moment and bit a cuticle. She said:

"I'll contact you in several days' time."

That's all she offered and it's all I took. I shook my head in agreement and stood up, extending my hand. She remained in the chair, and gingerly extended her own hand before guiding me out of the room with her eyes.

Outside the office, I quickly determined the direction of the exit and headed toward it, until I ran into a familiar shape. An Edmond-sized shape.

"Marsden, hold up for a minute."

It quickly became clear it wasn't an optional stop, and as I had just been booked by a rather comely client, I unclenched my right fist. He motioned over to an alcove next to the front entrance and tried his best to forcibly corner me.

"Now, listen to me-" I thought this was pretty childish, but I decided to hear him out. "I let Marie do what she needs to do. She is, well, she's quite unique. We've talked about it in the past, and came to the conclusion that I won't try to control her… behavior, as long as it doesn't affect me. We're pretty cordial about it at this point. I assume you'll treat her with all the respect you'd afford me."

He fondled my shoulder a bit too firmly at that point.

"More than I'd even afford you."

"I'm sure that wasn't an insult."

He stared into my eyes, trying to gauge how offended he should be, but I was giving him less than a bleached concrete wall.

"I think this whole thing is a waste of time you know."

"You mentioned that."

He fondled my shoulder again and I pulled away.

"Be careful with this. With her."

He tried to menacingly point his index at me, but men who make excuses for women have a way of defeating themselves. He shrank back into the murk as I made my way back out onto Hollywood Boulevard. I headed west.

2

Back outside it had just started to spit a few drops of rain. The lingering clouds crawled up the surrounding hills, as if someone was flooding the Los Angeles basin with heavy smoke. I felt the drops pelt various parts of my face before I sped up toward my apartment.

I couldn't really be sure what "behavior" Edmond was talking about. Maybe it was that Marie needed the freedom to make her own business decisions. It seemed more likely she needed the freedom to make other, more personal, decisions. I didn't have a lot of experience with men who willfully let their women play around, but it seemed like that's exactly what Edmond had just gone out of his way to reveal. As I tried to determine why Edmond had cornered me only to inform me of his less than faithful wife, I furtively touched the part of my coat which held the illicit photo of the younger sister. Then I checked my watch to find it to be just past six in the evening and realized I needed to eat, so I stopped in at a taco joint.

As I ate at the street-facing counter, I watched the sprinkling rain turn into more of a torrent. Taxi men dashed back to their cars to roll up the windows, others dashed for a departing bus. Of course there are always some that seem to take no notice of the rain at all and simply continue to drift down the street, without umbrella or presence.

California theoretically wasn't supposed to have weather like this. When it happened, it happened with drama and panache. Everyone was supposed to take notice.

I finished up, put my coat on and pulled it over my head into a makeshift canopy, before I stopped and remembered the picture again. I decided it better that my hair get wet rather than the picture with the naked girl on it, and shifted my coat back to its normal position. I stepped out into the rain and began to jog. The bronze stars inlaid in the slick ebony marble on the Walk of Fame were quite slippery, so after almost losing my balance on Ingrid Bergman, I checked myself and briskly walked the remaining two blocks, before turning down an unremarkable street and entering my building off Yucca.

As I stepped into the lobby, the blonde who lived next door stepped out of the elevator as it signaled its arrival with a solitary ding. I nodded at her; she nodded back with a contemptuous smile and continued to walk to the front door. I was evaluating the length of her pencil skirt when the elevator door closed. I hit the machined steel button for the third floor and checked my phone for messages. There were none.

On the third floor, I walked into my one-bedroom and unloaded my pockets onto the kitchen table. Of course the photo dominated the other baubles, so I decided to bend to my curiosity and examine the picture more carefully, without the inquisitive eyes of her older sister peeking over the picture and into my degenerate mind.

The young girl in the photo was exactly what one would think the kid sister of a dancer should look like, though noticeably more fragile than her older sibling. Like Mrs. Costello, every individual muscle in her milky white legs was toned. Her arms were thin, and led to pert, small breasts that looked like they were adequate in my estimation. Her face was almost jarring, as it wasn't so much beautiful as it was angular; her severe jaw led the eye directly up and back into her own eyes. They were the perfect width apart, separated by a small, proper nose. But her eyes, well her eyes were blue, very blue. Like her sister's, but sharper. The kind of blue you only see in tropical beer commercials and airline billboards. She was attractive alright.

Before letting my mind wander to more X-rated places, I reminded myself that I was supposed to impartially follow this girl and straightened myself out. I got up from the table, went over to the kitchen counter and mixed myself a gin and tonic. Cheap gin and ice with just a dash of tonic water would fuel my thinking as to how to approach the impending job, clearly.

I took my glass and strolled over to the window, which afforded me the view of a classic palm tree and a sliver of the rapidly darkening boulevard. I watched a bus slowly fill with people and noisily clatter off to its next stop before my mind went back to the photo.

She definitely didn't look happy, sad or titillated. I wondered what else was hidden behind those manipulatively-colored eyes until the phone rang. It was Quinlin:

"Ho! So, what's with you lately? Haven't had a drink in what, three weeks? You know I haven't even had a chance to make fun of your little car crash stunt yet, come on out."

"Usually need money to drink."

"Nonsense, I'll spot you tonight, we just wrapped a case."

"Successfully prosecuted another befuddled meth peddler, huh? Well that is unexpected, I'll give you that, but I got a date."

"Oh what's his name?" Quinlin's teasing was never subtle, and it never seemed to get old, for him at least.

"Technically it's for work, but I'll take what I can get. How about tomorrow?"

"Can't wait pal, give her one for me."

As abruptly as he entered, Quinlin left my consciousness, and I opted for a shower. As the steam slowly fogged the bathroom mirror, I undressed and stepped into the small stall. I continued to mull the composition of Stacy's photo, or at least the naked subject of said photo. Priorities, Marsden, priorities.

3

After my contemplative shower, I dressed myself and headed down to my dank, cave-like garage to retrieve my skillfully battered, but still classic German sedan. Over the years it had become clear to me that the older the car is, to a point, the more it'll blend into any street scene. No one notices the old heap, unless he's a car aficionado, but those are few and far between these days, or so the women in my life tell me.

On the way down the elevator stopped on the second floor, and the silent yet supercilious little guy who served as our maintenance man stepped in with a toolbox in one hand and a soda in the other. He gave his customary nod and leaned over just enough to glance the button for parking level two with his elbow.

In the garage, I walked over to my car and worked my way in under the wheel. I started her and she growled to life as I pointed for the exit.

Outside I rounded the corner, and then another; I took a right onto Hollywood Boulevard and started west. I took out the picture with the address on it and flipped it over in my lap. It read "Stacy" and then the address and apartment number. The girl lived in the flats around Crescent Heights and Santa Monica Boulevard. Time for some basic recon.

The clouds had miraculously evaporated, and it was another one of those California nights so nice it was impossible to describe to the jealous, out-of-state types. I watched the tall palms swoosh by as I motored over to Fairfax. Then, my phone started to ring. I had my suspicions about the number before I answered, so I decided to take a shot:

"Hello Mrs. Costello."

Bingo. She sounded slightly startled that I addressed her specifically, and just a tad intrigued: "Oh, hello Mr. Marsden. Do you have a second to chat?"

"I'm just on my way out in fact; toward your sister's."

"Wow, already getting started; I like that, but I'd like you to stop by my place first, it's very important."

I knew I made a questioning face at that instant, but of course she couldn't see it. I thought I heard another voice in the background. Maybe I wanted to be wrong about that.

"Now?"

"Is that possible?"

"Where are you located exactly?" I could've asked if we could just converse on the phone, but of course I didn't.

"Just off Fountain, almost at the end, in West Hollywood."

"Does Mr. Costello want to grill me some more about my ethics?"

"Oh, no, no. Of course not. He's not even here."

I must've paused for longer than I realized.

"Mr. Marsden?"

"Yes, ok, I can stop by. Just text me the address."

"Good. See you shortly."

A click-thud signaled she had hung up, so I did the same. I took a deep breath and looked at the newly arrived text; I turned right on Fountain and realized I was gripping the steering wheel as though it was the only thing keeping me from flying out the window. Of course I had met clients in their homes to go over cases and details, but this one felt different. She was beautiful, it was true, but she would already know I thought that. Women like her always know. The fact she failed to mention context and I failed to ask about it wasn't a good sign either.

■ ■ ■

She, or they, lived in a more modest abode than their customarily tony profession would lead one to expect. It was a two story Spanish complex with old-ish, cracking stucco adorning the outside. It had been renovated, but not recently. Still, it looked normal and unthreatening, like any other building in LA might.

I located a parallel spot and twisted the big car into it lovingly. Then I sat. I wasn't sure what to expect from an encounter like this. In other circumstances a man would make presumptions, and they'd be perfectly reasonable. I prided myself on my rationality, despite its rather weak overall influence on my actions.

Before I got too neurotic, I took a measured breath, checked my hair in the rearview and popped open the door. I stepped out into the comfortable night. A breeze tickled my neck as I locked the car and headed toward the complex. A few goosebumps dimpled my arms as I checked my phone again to verify the apartment number: 204.

I found a dark stairway headed upwards. The light had burnt out, or someone thought it'd be a hoot to make people blindly stumble up a dark flight of creaky steps. Always important to consider all the angles.

I reached the top of the treacherous stairs and found only one door. Two-zero-four was marked in faux gold letters in the center of the door. Each number had two tacks securing it. I noticed one was in need of some tapping as I formed my hand into a fist. My stomach felt too queasy for that time of night. I realized I should've stopped for a drink.

Just as I was thinking about which alcohol would be best for calming my nerves, my fist knocked on the door lightly three times. Nothing happened. I listened to the door and could hear soft classical music playing. Then, footsteps started approaching. It sounded like a small horse was charging at the other side of the door; it turned out not to be that. It was actually caused by stilettoes on hardwood.

As the door swung open, she caught me with my head down. I guess I had been trying to hear through my eyes, as now my eyes were most definitely focused on the fancy shoes, and the attached legs.

"Hello, detective."

My neck snapped upward like a bungee.

"Good evening Mrs. Costello."

She had changed her outfit. Now she wore the afore-mentioned shoes, a carefully adjusted plaid skirt that sat just above her knees, and a light blue blouse that was a little tighter than some would think appropriate, not that I was one of them.

It was the eyes that drew me in again though. They were little saucers of mind bending blue against her white satiny skin. This girl and her sister were quickly becoming the most beguiling-eye'd subjects I'd ever worked... for.

"Well, that was fast."

"I was in the neighborhood."

"I'm sure that's what you tell them all."

"I'm not sure to whom you're referring, Mrs. Costello."

She gave me a look a bird might make at a prowling cat. I leered just a smidge.

"Come in," she suggested.

I stepped inside. It was just like any other apartment I had visited, but this one had her in it.

"Drink?"

"Sure." Now was no time for fancy footwork. Pace yourself, Marsden.

I watched her waft across the room to a small bar cart that had several liquors which matched her vintage choice of cigarette.

She clinked an ice cube in each of two tumblers and then poured a dash of what appeared to be bourbon in each. She floated back over and handed me one.

"A woman who keeps bourbon in the bar. Very... elegant." I held my glass up briefly and took a measured drink.

She was in mid-taste as she semi-snorted a response. Endearing, is what a guy would say who was smitten.

"Remember, Mr. Marsden, you're here on business."

"No other reason I'd be here." I took what I deemed to be a graceful sip that involved just a bit too much booze, and shot her a faulty grin coupled with a grimace.

She looked like she'd seen the scene a million times before. A girl like her probably had.

"Alright Mrs. Costello, I'll take the bait. Why am I here?"

She sat down on the arm of the couch opposite where I sat. I could almost see up her skirt as she addressed me:

"I wanted to impress upon you how important this job is. Particularly because I know my husband accosted you on the way out today."

"Accosted is a little harsh I think, given... him."

She evaluated me for a moment, and began to think how to redress me and bring me back under her thumb after that slight. She couldn't; not reasonably. I could tell rationality was a cornerstone of hers as well, at least in her dreams. She said: "I'm not sure you're taking this seriously."

"When you contacted me, I was on the way to your sister's apartment, and not to enjoy the scenery." I was sure it sounded pretty moronic, and of course she picked right up on it.

"Clumsy, but I'll accept it." She took another sip and seemed to calm just a tick. "Do you find me attractive?"

That one caught me only a bit off-guard, despite my vast experience.

I responded: "Yes."

She took another drink and kept me in suspense, as an honorable girl is supposed to, though I wasn't sure how applicable that label was in this situation. She said:

"Why do you think I *really* invited you here? Say I had something more to ask of you–"

"I'm not sure I get what you're going for here Mrs. Costello." I couldn't crumble that easily.

"Yes you do."

She went over to refresh her drink and I swear twirled her skirt just a little, though at the time I hadn't eaten and had more to drink than I should've.

"Please make sure my sister is safe, that's all I ask."

She had turned around, leaned on the bar cart and stared at me through her glass. I had two moves, and I chose the right one, for the moment.

"Mrs. Costello, that's my main objective. Don't worry."

I finished my drink in one swish and stood up in the same moment; something not particularly wise. I took a small, awkward step and she was there to steady me.

"Are you alright?"

"Of course," I said.

I put my hands on both her lower shoulders and held her at a distance for a moment. Her eyes raked me up and down, then I could feel her muscles release their tension. I went in and aimed for the cheek, which I hit with my puckered lips.

She didn't flinch; I would have.

After she had shut the door I took a deep breath and admired my sense of morality. Of course it depended on whose side you were on to evaluate what had just happened. I was on the right track, according to myself.

My car purred to life as I adjusted myself in the driver's seat and set the radio according to my newfound brash mood. I checked my mirrors, nudged out of the parking spot and rolled around the corner onto another wide boulevard.

Had that meeting gone down exactly like it was supposed to? The other versions of the get-together banging around in my head annoyed me. I quickly came to the conclusion that my work for the night was done.

I decided on the scenic route and found myself meandering along the iconic and perpetually stimulating Sunset Boulevard. I could see a new batch of clouds moving in strategically from the coast and watched the street lights reflect off said clouds. Only a few people were privy to such situations as I was getting myself into. Gorgeous clients with dubious marital scruples who invite you over for cocktails… why not? That must've been some high proof optimism I had just imbibed.

Ten minutes later and I'd made my way up onto Hollywood Boulevard. After a few blocks I made a left and stowed myself back in my apartment complex. Another safe journey home, despite my wandering mind. At least my car still had her head in the game; she'd always be my mistress. I stared a moment at the polished chrome, locked her and made for the elevator lobby. Every man needs his rock, or in LA, a loyal car, I thought to myself, reveling in my solitude.

Another ten minutes and I was fluffed into my enormously comfortable bed. It obviously wasn't the night to pursue the case; fate and Mrs. Costello had showed me that and then some.

4

If you want a consistently rude and indecisive wake up routine, make sure to live in a city. Even one as pleasantly spread out as Los Angeles has a ready supply of trash trucks and nail gun-wielding air-breathers to ensure no one sleeps past the apparently agreed upon 9 a.m. start time. Unfortunately, I'd never been able to get on board with such an arbitrary timetable.

Yet again I was awoken by construction in the next lot over, or I thought I was, until I was awoken again by the trill of my phone. After jostling everything on the nightstand and sending several items flying with some wrist flicks, I found the phone and answered.

"Good morning, Mr. Marsden!" The voice tried too hard to be nice.

"Hello Quin."

"Ah, you're up, barely. Meet me for lunch."

"Breakfast."

"It'll probably be liquid either way at this hour. State House in twenty?"

"Optimistic, but I'll make it happen."

"Of course you will." I could see the mocking smile bubbling up through the small holes in the speakerphone.

The line went dead and my lids started to droop again, so I kicked my feet out over the edge of the bed and tried to lurch myself into a more vertical position. After some huffing and puffing and half-hearted self-encouragement, I left the bedroom and hit the bathroom for some superficial self-buffing. I had just enough time to drink a tall glass of orange juice and butter one piece of crackly, unpleasant toast before dashing out the door.

My meeting with Mrs. Costello the night before meant exactly nothing. That's what I had decided by the time I reached the elevator. I had gleaned next to nothing in terms of new details, and other than that, had come up with a lot of thigh and not much else.

Once in the elevator, I again headed down to my garage, settled into the driver's seat, donned a pair of the perfunctory California shades and slipped out into the glare.

Hollywood is one of those funny places where you can live among throngs of tourists and feel lucky that you live in a place other people think of as a vacation spot. For a while.

After puzzling my way around several artificial traffic jams caused solely by terrible, probably visiting, drivers, I finally swung onto Highland Avenue. A few minutes later I found myself drifting down Melrose opposite State

House, and spotted Quinlin Halle deliberately dawdling outside the door speaking with the pretty hostess. I also noticed the suspiciously shiny green Jag parked a few spots down from the entrance. The damned LA native always found the best spot. I resigned myself to a spot two lengthy blocks away, and quickly jogged down the sidewalk to sidle up next to my chortling friend.

He said to the hostess: "If only I wasn't engaged... how old are you darlin'?"

He winked at her and shot a knowing glance at me as we followed her colleague into the dining portion of the establishment. The light was hazy grey, due to tinted windows that were supposed to provide atmosphere. It was one of the last places in Los Angeles where one could smoke inside unmolested, legally at least. As it turned out, we provided the most atmosphere the deserted place could stand that early in the day. Quinlin found a table he liked, beckoned me to sit down, and menus magically appeared.

"Well I'm glad the engagement hasn't destroyed your libido. How many years has it been now?"

"It'll be eight this May, and she couldn't be happier." Quin took a long gulp of water. "We only get one life; I don't need to tell you. Should explain all the goings on, if you will."

"I won't, but I get it."

Quinlin Halle was exactly what you'd want in a confidant. He was stocky, just bulbous enough to be trustworthy, and wiser than, well, a younger man. I'd exposed

the district attorney's investigator to plenty of my she-
nanigans and gotten merely a snide remark and a drink
for most of them.

"Well I'm going for the Cohiba. Yourself?"

He simultaneously offered the menu and server up to
me.

"I'll go with the same."

"Two scotch and sodas too."

There was no use arguing with an order for alcohol
from Quinlin. You were to drink and enjoy. I never had a
problem obliging.

The small, sweaty man tasked with handling us scam-
pered off in search of our tobacco selection. It was almost
quaint in this day and age, if it wasn't for the price. Quin
took a deep breath and seemed to sink into his chair oh so
slightly as I watched.

"So, detective business treating you well again I
guess."

"Why do you say that?"

"Well we're meeting today as opposed to yesterday,
no?" He took another deep breath and waited respectfully
for a response.

I looked out the artfully tinted windows.

"Not well, but I'll take what I can get. This one could
get juicy."

The sweaty little man returned with two cigars and
two short glasses filled with scotch and fizzling soda.

"I'm sure. Blackmail as usual?"

"You always guess that when I say juicy."

He took a sip of his drink and swallowed authoritatively, as was expected. His two chins took a minute to settle down.

I said: "This one seems to be slightly more complicated than that. Or my wallet would hope." "Yeah" he responded, less than impressed.

I filled him in about the ballerina, her unconventional marriage and her younger sister, leaving out names where required. He snorted and took another fizzling sip.

I said: "So yeah, might be blackmail, but might be something more." I never liked connecting all the dots for Quinlin; I'd learned that some grey area was always a good idea with him.

He said: "Sounds like yet another case of sex on the mind to me."

"Whose mind?"

He took another long sip, snipped the tip of his premium cigar, put a match to the end and puffed a few times to light it. The stogie flared as he launched:

"You know sex is one of the only things humans do reliably well."

I guffawed politely and snipped my own cigar.

"I don't mean it as a joke this time. Sex is the thing that keeps humanity around, so some people must do it reliably well. And of course, since it's such an accessible—and pleasurable—behavior, people will try to do it as much as possible, which in turn means there are going to be some dubious pitfalls." He said it like a scientist dissecting a frog; he prodded it a bit. I let it lie. "Just make sure you're not the one falling in the pit."

I lit my cigar and took several over-exaggerated puffs to get it going respectably. I looked up at him, but he was busy looking at the ornately constructed tin ceiling.

He said: "My advice on this one would be to play conservative, but that's just because I'd like to keep you around for a little while longer."

"That sounds like a sensitive cop-out," I offered graciously.

He took another puff, adjusted his collar and shut me down: "I know a possible train wreck when I see one Marsden. Remember, I'm just slightly older than you."

He ruffled his wrinkles, made his age apparent as he always did, and continued: "Sounds like you don't have all the information about these dames yet. Don't get worried by tits, there're plenty of them to go around."

Satisfied with his assessment, he took another puff of his fancy cigar and inquired how my real love life was going. I assured him it was stalled out as I finished my own cigar. I then downed my remaining, only slightly useful scotch and bid him adieu.

Before I could exit, Quinlin remarked that he was only out to help, and immediately took a long swig of his drink. I took that to mean he was still trustworthy and headed towards the door. There's only so much a friend can teach you, and even then, you have to listen.

5

Back in the car, I motored down Melrose toward Stacy's. Between lights I tried to reconcile Quin's advice, Stacy's reported ill-repute and Marie Costello's legs. Frankly, none of them got me closer to any sort of conclusion, so I adjusted the radio to something more enthusiastic and sped faster toward Santa Monica and Crescent Heights.

The complex was, surprise, a Spanish stucco number; but this time it looked like someone had tried too hard to make it real, opting instead for authentic fake. The beams that jutted from beneath the eves were painted a particularly unpleasant sort of brown, meant to represent wood apparently. On either side of the main entrance were two large light fixtures, which were trying to be historically accurate.

I checked the parking signs, noted that my car would not be street-sweepered away this late in the afternoon and pulled up opposite the complex, about five car lengths down from the front entrance. I began the stakeout, waiting for my quarry to make her first appearance. It's true I was theoretically being paid to sit around, but it was the worst kind of sitting: anxious sitting. And there wasn't even a ton of planning to hash out. I had been a little short with Mrs. Costello that first day regarding how to best track Stacy's movements, but that was only for business; she had been right in this case. The best way to figure out this particular girl's story was to follow her from home to wherever and back.

The sky was beginning to dim, and the slightest hint of the curious scent of night was starting to seep out of the jasmine, when someone other than the mailman or water delivery guy caught my attention. I noticed the small palms planted on either side of the building's entrance rustle slightly as a thin, harried girl carefully bounced down the stairs and across the street to an atrociously boring blue Chrysler convertible. She was wearing a long sleeve white dress with small black polka-dots, which ended at her mid-thigh. A pair of black leather ankle boots seemed to weigh down her lithe legs. Her hair was up in a girlish ponytail.

If I was by the book, I should've checked her against my photo, but I figured I'd already spent quite a few billable hours examining Stacy's photo and decided to give myself the benefit of the doubt.

She started the car and seemed to instantaneously speed off in the opposite direction than the way I was oriented. After she had passed the four way stop behind me down the street, I sparked the motor and executed a precise U-turn to take chase. She headed up Crescent Heights and into the hills just as the setting sun was turning the sky a painfully beautiful tangerine color. About two miles after crossing Sunset, she took a jerky left and started a switch back route into the depths of the Hollywood Hills. She wound up in a tunnel of eucalyptus trees as I followed about one turn behind.

As we gained altitude the trees began to thin. The road was barely wide enough for one car, let alone the so-called traffic that prowled LA. It was bordered on one side by what seemed to be a sheer wall of dirt and brown, desiccated brush, while the other side simply dropped away down the hills, a house or two precariously clipped to the side of the incline. Just as I was wondering how this part of town had not burst into inextinguishable flames years ago, I turned and found myself about a hundred yards back from the convertible. It was moving forward, but very tentatively. I assumed she was scanning for a street spot, but was instantly proven incorrect as she made a sharp left into a vacant driveway attached to an ostensibly expensive house.

I coasted past just as she was exiting her car. She coiffed her hair a bit and appeared to pause to take a breath before my forward motion brought an aptly named privacy hedge into my line of sight. I cursed under my breath and concentrated on my own parking now that I knew her destination.

A more patient detective would now sit on the subject until she reemerged, and try to mock up a schedule and destination list before trying to suss out the purpose of her visit. But not me. Of course I couldn't be the guy who just quietly sat in the car and billed hours.

I found a place to park one bend up the street and casually walked back down toward the house.

It was a mid-century special that hadn't been well maintained. It could've been a jewel, but instead was more of a muddy pebble. The front yard was surrounded by a thick, unkempt privacy hedge, and it looked like the bushy lawn had maybe been trimmed two summers ago. The windows were single pane originals, and there appeared to be more split, dried paint flecks on the stoop than on the door where they evidently originated. I didn't doubt the house was worth quite a bit over a million at this point, though no one would be able to tell you exactly why.

As I peered around the hedge, the only light was coming through the front main picture window. The light was filtering out through venetian blinds, and plastered horizontal bars of light across the quickly darkening front yard. I was a little taken aback by what I saw next.

Stacy was mounted on a sort of sarcophagus. She was completely naked except for the brilliantly shiny staff she suggestively held out in her right hand. Her expression was blank at first, then she appeared to follow something out of my view around the room with only her eyes, until she smiled an apparently acceptable amount. Three flashes went off quickly, and then a dark figure's back appeared through the window partially obscuring the girl. She tried to steady herself on his shoulder, but he batted it away. Then, he roughly grabbed her right inner knee and bent her leg outward slightly. She winced. He then moved the staff between her thighs exactly where a pornography consumer would want it, and I watched a pallor spread across her face.

I should've just observed or I should've left. I did neither.

As stealthily as I felt I could, I used flat fleet and sprinted towards the front door. I hit it perfectly square with my shoulder, which did about as much good as a toothpick spearing a concrete wall. I bounced back a foot or so, but not before the dark shape from before cracked the door to see who his visitor was.

My shoulder was through the open door, and his face, so fast he didn't even have time to register a yelp, let alone a question. As I plowed through, Stacy dropped her staff and steadied herself on the top of the sarcophagus. Her blue eyes were so wide you could've lost a schooner in their depths, but her lips remained just so pursed. I realized she wasn't blinking, and her bobbing head looked like a balloon attached to her shoulders; she must've been on something. Something good.

I swiveled my head back around and found the dark shape to be slightly wider than I was expecting. The man whose face was now mostly pulp was about five foot eight and clearly balding. He wore a sort of tunic that most would scoff at as ridiculous, including me. He wore brown suede beetle boots and dark denim pants that were tight for a woman at least half his age, not to mention weight.

Blood poured from his nose and from a gash above his right eye. He tried to stem the flow with his plump fingers, but the blood decided it wanted out regardless and trickled down past his wrist. He was still able to stammer though.

"Who are you?? What is this?"

I took a moment to survey the room to ensure there weren't any threats; plus it meant I could ignore him a few moments longer.

There was a fancy camera set up next to the bleeding man. It was aimed at what did in fact appear to be a model of a sarcophagus, and one quivering, naked girl. The rest of the room looked like it hadn't been updated for at least ten years, which was curious, since the consumers of pornography in this day and age demand relevance and realism, or so I'm told.

"What is the meaning of this?" The bleeding heap was talking again, and I had a feeling I had to respond or I'd be subject to more. I turned back to him sporting a gruff look and a little swagger.

A shot rang out before I could open my mouth and somehow more blood poured from the already badly damaged man's face. I took a dive, and just in time, as another shot rang out, whizzed through the space where I had just been standing and punched through the picture window in the front of the room. As the window was shattering, I could see the girl deliberately tumble off the prop and take cover behind it, hugging her knees.

And then there was nothing.

I expected more attempts but was wrong; it was just the two shots, then silence. I slowly panned past the now clearly dead pornographer and settled on the teary-eyed naked girl who stared right back at me. Simultaneously I heard some heavy steps down what I guessed was a back stairway and a car start and vroom away. Then all I could hear was the breeze rustling the geraniums in the busted front window's planter box.

I slowly raised my head and confirmed that no one else was targeting anyone with any guns. I raised my finger to my lips and made sure the girl saw me. She nodded through her big eyes and I started assessing the damage.

There was one dead man, another living man with a sore shoulder, a living girl and a suspected pornography studio. There were more bullets around than I cared for.

Without knowing exactly what I was looking for, I started a cursory investigation of the premises. I stumbled into a dark kitchen. It smelled of stale, day old breakfast. I clicked the lights on and found it to be aesthetically outdated like the rest of the house but otherwise empty, and moved on down the central back hall, which was all darkness. I felt along the walls and found three doors.

Inside the first on the left was what appeared to be a storage room. I took out my phone to use as a flashlight. From the number of dusty breasts I saw on the documents contained in the moth-ridden cardboard boxes, I assumed it was what could euphemistically be called an archive. Besides the boxes, there was a small step ladder and old cleaning supplies, most of which were paradoxically filthy.

I moved back into the hallway and tried the door direct-ly across the way. This room was plain white, and had a striped mattress with a tripod and digital camcorder set up facing it. When I had first glimpsed the illicit picture of Stacy, it had struck me that still-photos were a bit outdated. That picture was probably only a preview for other more sordid media, if this second setup was any indication.

Finally I gently padded back into the hall and tried the end door. It was a little stiff, but I put some more pres-sure on it and got it open. This bedroom looked respect-able enough for someone to actually live in. Perhaps not a reputable man, but someone. The comforter cover on the king-size bed was a deep plum color, which I could make out thanks to a dim bedside reading lamp that had been left on, perhaps for mood. There were more flowers than one would expect in a man's room, but then again this was a man who wore tunics.

Next to the bed was a nightstand, and arrayed under the window along the wall were several official-looking locking filing cabinets.

I started with the easily accessible nightstand. The top drawer contained the usual expired medications and boring reading material one might find in anyone's top drawer. The bottom drawer contained the usual naughty and titillating sexual instruments you'd find in a pornog-rapher's house.

Breathing deep, I shut both and moved onto the locked filing cabinets. As with most cheap filing cabinets, the trick to these was the lock at the top, which locked all the other drawers below it. I took out my small pocket knife, selected a small pick and went to work on the lock.

With half finesse and half muscle, I ripped open the top drawer, which was very neatly organized. There were folders marked A-F, and each one seemed to contain portfolios of various "models." While entertaining, there was nothing particularly interesting, except for one extraordinarily roughed up folder marked "Acquisitions." I saw something I liked, and didn't like.

A porcelain white, sculpted calf protruded from the tattered folder.

I gingerly grasped the photo with what existed of my fingernails and pulled it out slowly, separating it from about half a dozen others. A much younger version of a familiar, perfectly worked lower leg connected to an ideally proportioned upper thigh appeared. I pulled more and found her to be wearing nothing else that might obscure her form. As I extracted the entire photo, it looked a lot like a very young ballerina; too young.

For a moment I froze, wondering what to make of the discovery. What was she doing in this dive, and why did this corpse have so many pictures of her that appeared to be so old? I was sure there was a complicated reason for these pictures to be in this man's house, but I wasn't sure I wanted to find out; my brain hurt.

Before I put too much thought into it, I grabbed the photos I could and stashed them in my leather jacket's inner pocket. One slipped to the floor and I noticed on the back the word "Upton" scrawled loosely in black pencil.

I retrieved it, put it with the others, patted them carefully through the worn leather and stood up, scanning the only window in the room. There was still no movement.

I walked carefully back into the main room. Stacy was still cowering next to the fake sarcophagus. As I approached, I noticed tears had made little streams down the front of her taut face. I stared her down as best I could given the circumstances, then tried to make an approach. She flinched and I froze again.

Without a word I excused myself from the situation and slinked back into the dead pornographer's bedroom. I found an emerald green robe and draped it over my arm and put on my best valet act.

Back in the living room I approached again and presented the robe carefully in her direction. Seemingly without moving she accepted the offering and draped herself in the rough terrycloth of his sub-par bathrobe. I stood up and adjusted myself. She slowly fell onto her side and bunched the robe on her chest.

"Alright, it's time to go." I waited and hoped I hadn't triggered any more tears.

"What about-" she weakly pointed toward the splayed body of her dead photographer.

"He doesn't matter. Your sister sent me."

She hesitated, then put her insubstantial weight on one arm and stood up. She appeared to teeter before I caught her shoulders. I looked at the only thing anyone would; her eyes.

They were bordered with gently trembling lashes and contained those terrifyingly persuasive blue irises. The glinting was almost mesmerizing enough to make me forget she was a naked human girl significantly younger than myself. Then I looked vaguely to her left and noted the corpse of the pornographer. This focused me.

"Alright Stacy, we have to go, now."

"What?" She looked like she was trying to focus about a hundred yards behind me.

I took that to mean she was still doped up. I grasped her chin firmly in my right hand, which I felt was pretty compelling.

I said: "We have to leave here right now. I'll bring you to your sister."

"You can't!" Her turquoise blue eyes blinked and then started to tear up again. I grabbed her by the collar, but melted.

"Why not?"

"Please, I promise I won't cause any more trouble. I'll do anything."

I thought to myself for a moment, and realized she had just uttered the phrase that had baffled men for centuries. Unfortunately, I was a man.

"Fine. But we have to leave here. Come on."

I carefully took her hand and clutched it like I would a rare flower. We made our way outside and stopped at the end of the drive.

"Gimmie a minute." Before she could object, I released her hand and made for the front door. She didn't follow and I relaxed a degree or so.

I reentered the house and looked for clues of myself. The only things I could see were a corpse and an illuminated sarcophagus. A large DSLR camera sat on a tripod aimed at the sarcophagus. Trying to minimize my handling of it, I managed to get the memory card door open and slipped the card out of the camera. Then I buffed off the camera with my sleeve. I glanced down the hall, made sure no lights where left on and headed for the front door. I clicked the security lock, made sure the door handle locked behind me, wiped the knob and slinked out as stylishly as possible.

Ascending the driveway, I still heard no disturbance in the neighborhood. However, I soon came upon the shivering little girl. She had her arms crossed in the robe and was at least sober enough to show her discontent.

"What did you just do?" I could tell she was trying to protect herself, but didn't know a damned thing about it.

I took her hand again. She tried to retract it, but I didn't let her.

Instead I pulled her slightly closer. Her eyes impossibly got wider. I breathed on her, and she returned the gesture.

Before she could speak, I started pulling her up the street toward my car. At first she tried to protest, but then I saw her resolve suddenly vanish.

As if we were in the forecourt of the Peninsula hotel, I opened the passenger door for her before she could react and motioned her inside. She paused, then carefully positioned herself on the passenger seat. She would've been beautiful, if it wasn't for the circumstances.

I slammed the door, adjusted my collar, and chose to take the route behind the car to the driver's side. When I got there I slowed as my hand touched the cold metal door handle; I had just witnessed a murder and perhaps more. I wondered why I'd just risked everything for this girl. I looked skyward and found nothing but stars. There aren't even supposed to be real stars in Los Angeles.

My knuckles cracked as I opened the door and slid into the driver's seat. Stacy sat perfectly still in the passenger seat; a statue would've been envious of her posture.

I turned the key and the V8 roared to life like a jet engine. I applied some pressure to the gas pedal and drove away from the lascivious stiff's residence, down the hill toward West Hollywood. Stacy remained motionless and grey until we descended past Sunset. Her eyes drooped now and again.

The moon was just passing what I considered to be the tipping point when she piped up:

"So, what's going to happen now?"

I was legitimately interested as to whether she would answer her own question: "What do you mean?"

"Come on, what are you going to tell my sister? And the police?"

I took the requisite deep, introspective breath and replied:

"I was hired by your sister... so what do you want them to know?"

She was taken aback by this, as she thought I had her. She responded: "I'm sorry."

I waited for her to add to her testimony, but it was in vain. She looked at me with her Vegas pool eyes and the last of my moxie evaporated. After about fifteen minutes, we were back in front of her humble complex.

I was feeling generous: "Alright, I won't take you to your sister, but will you stay here, so we can contact you if we need to?"

She replied absolutely: "Okay."

I looked at her, and a granite impression of her gazed back. My stomach churned and I knew I no longer could influence the outcome of this particular situation. It was fifty-fifty that I'd ever even see the girl again, but I didn't have the energy to come up with a better plan. Taking Stacy to her older sister would only embroil the ballerina unnecessarily in a murder. Besides, something obviously more important involving Marie was simmering in the primal part of my brain.

I unlocked the doors and she appeared to straighten herself up. She groomed some stray hair strands back and smoothed where the robe hid the intersection of her legs. I breathed out heavily, "It's not so bad; it could be worse."

She shot me a look, a pretty haughty look for a girl in her condition, then scooted out of the car and walked toward the building entrance as though she was traipsing down a stretch of red carpet. It couldn't have been all for my benefit, but nobody else was there. I watched the terrycloth robe retreat behind the plate glass doors. I audibly sighed; it was my only recourse.

6

On the way back to Hollywood I cranked my stereo louder than I should have, since I really should've been trying to focus and figure out my next move. I had just witnessed a murder, almost become murder victim myself, found a young naked girl and a whole bunch of mysterious, explicit pictures of her older sister, all under the roof of a scummy smut dealer.

Instead I opted to listen to the music and try to concentrate on the road. Every electric string plucked in the early seventies rock reverberated a few times up and down my spine, finally finding a home vibrating in my brain; they caused ripples to flow through my mental image of Mrs. Costello.

I couldn't shake what had transpired though. I had compromised my own common sense, sounded the amateur-hour alarm and barged into an investigation because of my feelings. Plus there was the assault on the fat porn producing oaf. Or maybe, I had just been acting to prevent something worse from happening to the poor girl, although that would probably be too convenient.

Then again, as I had reminded myself several times when dealing with this particular pair of females, I was just a man. Of course I was going to be prone to stupid decisions. I moved on and tried to debrief myself about the incident. I soon decided that whoever was there to kill the pornographer had not expected me to be there as well, because how could he? The crime scene was still intact otherwise, so perhaps my not informing the police immediately would be acceptable. Wishful thinking from a tired man.

After the rickety gate had finished clinking along its track, I stowed my car back under my building and ascended to my floor. It felt like the air in the elevator weighed a thousand pounds, which made it pretty difficult to breathe.

Once inside my apartment, I locked the door behind me and went straight for the bourbon. I plunked one rock into a tumbler and drowned it with liquor. Outside, a few stray cars and people slowly slid by on Hollywood Boulevard. I checked the clock. Three-thirty a.m. meant the bars had closed about an hour and a half before, which meant the action was over for the night. I leaned against the window as I sipped my drink.

Before I had a chance to finish all of it, I dialed Quin's number and was on ring number three before he picked up. He sounded like you'd expect a man who shouldn't be awake at that hour would sound.

"Quin, there's been a situation I think you should be aware of."

"Sex on the mind, what did I tell you?"

"Well it's that case anyway. Someone has probably been taken advantage of... and someone has been killed."

A few snorts followed and I assumed he had just sat up in bed, though he still maintained the sleep in his voice, just in case I was kidding.

"What happened?"

I told him everything that had transpired in the pornographer's house.

He perked up, but wasn't happy: "You know that me knowing all this could be a problem; that wasn't smart."

"Well the whole setup is kind of out there, I didn't want to involve a whole bunch of cops who didn't understand the situation, or my participation in it. The crime scene is still there and there's still the small issue of a murderer running around. Too many people know, including the girl. I haven't really got a bead on her yet."

"They're gonna sweat you for this."

"Probably."

There was nothing but slow breathing on the other end of the line. I took another swig of my drink.

"Did you kill him?" Quinlin's curiosity sounded genuine.

"He probably deserved it, but no, I didn't."

I could see him nodding understandingly in my head. I hoped he was doing the same thing for real on the other end of the line.

"Well it'll give you some bonus points that you report-ed it, but you reported it to me and not the cops, that's going to be a problem… for you."

"Well, my next few days are clear."

"Good," he almost snarled through the phone. Then he hung up. I didn't expect him to kiss me on the forehead and tuck me in, but then again at this point I wouldn't have turned him down. Things were going to get rough.

It was in fact probably a terrible idea to call Quin; I wasn't really sure what had prompted me to do so. An anonymous tip would've achieved the same result in practice, in terms of getting a police investigation going. Continuing to stare out at the empty boulevard, I started to believe that perhaps I'd made a move to the liquor too quick, and my judgment was off. Then the alcohol pulled the rug out from under that idea and planted another: I supposed I'd had a feeling Quinlin in particular should be involved for this one, and now he was. I didn't have many friends in town at the moment. I wondered what my bal-lerina would think.

7

The next morning I was surprised to find myself not in jail. I woke up to a flock of crows sitting on the lovely rosemary bush outside my window in the adjacent yard. It got me wondering why this group had chosen to graze there as opposed to scrounging on the trash strewn Hollywood Boulevard that lay one block beyond. It looked like they were enjoying some small berries.

My head ached and I didn't think it was just due to the alcohol I'd consumed before dozing off. I stretched, lumbered out of bed and attempted to dress myself respectably. Two pieces of crackly toast later I was in the car and on the road. It was a gamble, but my only task for the day was waiting for the police, so I felt I could be a bit liberal with my schedule.

About fifteen minutes later I arrived outside the ballerina's apartment. The venetian blinds were drawn, which told me she was either asleep or away. In other words, a useless observation as we say in the trade. I wondered if I should've driven over after all.

On her street, I noted that of course permit parking was in effect that early in the day, so I gave the motor a little kick and puttered down around the corner, to park on a wide boulevard. My space was in front of a fancy coffee shop. I pondered if there were more ways I could delay this meeting, perhaps with a cup of coffee, which I rarely drank.

I didn't get the chance to finish that thought, as Mr. Costello appeared, walking into the coffee shop. At first I was concerned he'd spotted me, until I realized his focus was on a man already sitting at a small circular table inside. I couldn't tell how tall the new man was, because he was seated, but he was definitely older, and had shiny grey hair with a few dashes of soot left from a generation ago. He sat perched rigidly upright in his chair, a posture which looked uncomfortable. His jaw shuddered just slightly, although he wasn't saying or eating anything. Intensity flowed from his dark, squinted eyes, but couldn't completely draw attention away from his pronounced chin.

Costello daintily took a seat opposite the man and sat back a bit. The older man seemed to lean forward to take up the slack and started talking, his lips the only thing moving on his otherwise frozen frame. Words seemed to visibly tear into Costello's skin, and sweat began to appear on his brow and under his eyes. He was clearly being berated, in a very controlled fashion.

Before Costello could open his mouth in defense, the old man stood up and pushed in his chair deliberately. He was taller than I expected, at about six foot two. He wasn't quite as gaunt as he appeared when he was coiled up on the chair either. He looked eerily familiar.

The old man exited the shop and immediately stomped across the street and around a corner. I hadn't even noticed that Costello had also vacated his seat. He walked out the front door and stopped. His eyes seemed to focus on infinity for a moment, before I watched him walk away, not toward, the Costello residence.

My car door had already slammed firmly shut when I realized I had gotten out, put on my jacket from the night before, and was staring down the street toward Mrs. Costello's house. Without hesitation I started forcefully walking towards it. I passed a woman and her rodent-esque dog, then I passed an ancient man who was somehow still creaking along with his cane.

I stepped up to the bottom of the dark staircase and paused. If I had been sophisticated, I would've taken out a cigarette, artfully lit it and used it to steel myself. Instead I just got out my phone and dialed her number.

Mrs. Costello answered on the first ring. She beckoned that I come up before I could get out any real words.

Thirty seconds later I was standing outside her door. I observed the grain of the wood under the flaking paint, then tried to figure out how I was going to broach the subject at hand, before reprimanding myself for not thinking about it before calling her. I knocked.

She answered the door almost instantly. She was wearing a tight, blank grey t-shirt and a pair of fraying but extremely flattering short white shorts. A small bead of sweat trickled down her forehead.

"Well this is rather unexpected."

She wiped away the sweat nonchalantly.

"Is it?" My mind was moving too quickly to be creative.

I walked past her and decided on the couch. I took a seat. She shut the door behind me, though I got the feeling she wished I hadn't invited myself in so quickly.

She inquired very innocently: "Is there a problem with my sister's case?"

I didn't reply. I'd always prided myself on having a flair for the dramatic.

I reached into my jacket pocket and clutched the photos I had obtained the previous night. Before she could ask anything else, I threw the photos as haphazardly as possible all over her coffee table. Her eyes turned into pie plates as naked skin splashed over the table and I could see her lips part just a millimeter or two. Then she flushed red and tried to speak, but couldn't.

I said what didn't need to be said: "That, Mrs. Costello, is you."

PART II

The Pool

8

She froze and stared at me. Her wide, unfairly opalescent eyes shimmered, then seemed to focus just slightly above and past my head. Before Mrs. Costello could attempt a recovery, I made a dash for the liquor I'd noticed on my previous visit. The pictures I'd found were definitely of her; I'd know that physique anywhere. It was her turn to make a play.

I had plunked a few cubes into some short glasses when the interaction resumed.

She started: "No they're not. Of course not. I've never seen those pictures before in my life."

"Yes, they are."

I finished my recipe of alcohol and ice and spun around slowly, one in each hand. She stood much closer than I was expecting.

"Mr. Marsden, I don't know what you're talking about." They always say the same thing.

I looked back into her eyes, which were now glazed in a glossy shroud of what I took to be nascent tears. I held out one of the drinks. She took it.

I made my way back over to the uncomfortable, low-backed couch and took a seat once again. I sipped as I watched her slowly turn towards me and sip her own drink. It was like watching a very confused, pretty little girl. She crossed her arms tightly across her chest, still holding onto the glass, as I went on to describe the scene at Talbot's the night before, and the condition of her sister.

Her voice waivered, "but is she really alright? Maybe I should go over there and-"

I was feeling bold and wasn't going to let her get away: "I know it's you in the pictures. The question is why this shady guy had pictures of you, and why he was after getting the same from your sister." Another sip, longer this time. It was warranted.

Without warning she downed her drink in a gulp and turned away from me. She seemed to be completely in control, but I could never be sure with her.

She said: "I only employed you to look after my sister."

"You employed me to find out what was going on. I found pictures of you in the course of my investigation. They're obviously significant."

It was meant to be presumptuous. Regardless, I wasn't sure where I was going with it.

She spun back around and got down on her knees in front of me. I could see just a hint of a tear in one ocean-blue eye, then she hit below the belt: She put her hand on my left thigh. My good thigh.

She said: "I'm not sure what to start with."

"This job is going to be impossible without the full truth Mrs. Costello."

At that point she started to shake just a bit. Her thumb and other fingers tightened around my thigh. The skeptic in me knew the theatrics were probably misdirection, but I decided to tolerate it.

Before she could do more, I pulled her up onto the couch and sat her next to me. Then I leaned in and my lips touched hers without hesitation. I didn't know what I was doing... and then I did.

I felt the dry cracks in her lips as my tongue passed over them. She tried to recoil just enough for me to pull her tighter. She closed her eyes and opened her mouth wider and that was that. She went limp and my hands started roving. I knew this was not the type of detecting I was being paid for. The problem was, I wasn't even that drunk. Right?

9

Later in the afternoon, she got up to check her phone. The naked form I had only seen in photographs prior to that day floated over to it and frowned just slightly as she declared that no news from Mr. Costello meant he wouldn't be home anytime soon. I didn't ask any questions, which was odd, given what I had seen in the coffee shop earlier and my propensity to ruin nice situations.

She replaced the phone on the faux-oak dresser, turned and did what I imagined must be considered a little stretch in the dance world. Arching her back, she extended one of her long legs out in front of her at forty five degrees. While it's true I didn't know anything about ballet, I did know a little something about legs.

She relaxed and came back toward me. There was something about the way she moved that was not so much aesthetic as curious. It looked like she felt every mechanical component of her gait with each step. She worked to make her walk beautiful. As a detective, I appreciated such a high level of meticulousness. As a man I also liked it.

She slinked back to the bed and seemed to float onto her back. I didn't have a choice at that point. I looked down between her creamy thighs and found yet more perfection. She was supple and tasted fantastic. I licked my lips. No one else could ever taste like that. A part of my brain registered that it was chemical luck, that I found her so pleasurable. But it was fate too. After a while I migrated up and she pulled me inside her. There are a million ways to describe that level of ecstasy, and she summed them all up in a slight purr as our movements became more rhythmic. I tried to take in the whole scene; it was perfect. It looked perfect, felt perfect, smelled perfect. Our limbs intermingled and we fit together like a bespoke jigsaw puzzle. It had to mean something.

■ ■ ■

The next thing I officially remembered was waking up the next morning. I was sore in the right places, but also in the head. Theoretically I should've taken stock of the situation, as there were probably several ethical dilemmas to address. But all I could focus on were the ivory shoulders of the ballerina next to me.

Her eyes slid open and looked at me nonchalantly. I was getting too used to those eyes.

"Mrs.-"

She interrupted thoughtfully: "Upton."

"I'm not sure-"

"I am. My name is Marie Upton. And I'm not really married, not truly." She turned her gaze away from me and placed her head delicately back on the neighboring pillow.

"Well I suppose that's a slight improvement."

"No, it's not." She turned back and gave me a look my hapless third grade teacher might have given if I spoke out of turn. I laid my hand on her pale, soft back and tried to change the mood. But I was only a smart-ass detective again.

She said: "Mr. Marsden, you were correct. Those pictures are of me."

"I know."

"Before you get too ahead of yourself, I want to warn you that I'm not paying you to look into me, I just want my sister to be alright."

"Who took the photos of you? Why would some schmuck like Talbot have them?"

She clammed up and reached for what turned out to be a pack of her filter-less cigarettes and a lighter. She lit one out of my view, then said:

"You know I'm the nothing."

"Way to be melodramatic. What does that mean?"

"Stacy was at Westlake University. She was going after her nursing degree."

"That's admirable. Did she drop out?"

"Yup," she took a puff and blew the smoke out authoritatively.

"Why?"

"I don't know."

"Yes you do." I placed my left hand in the crook of her bare neck. I toyed a little. She didn't seem to mind.

"No, I don't. About a year ago she just stopped. She came to me in tears but didn't say why."

"Did something happen at school?"

"She claimed nothing happened, of course." She took another puff and I slid the sheet covering her down an indecent amount.

"Did your parents say anything? Did she tell them anything?"

"I talked to my mother about it, but she claimed that Stacy hadn't said anything and I have no reason to doubt her."

"What about your father?" She jerked her head up and her whole body seemed to go rigid.

"Is something wrong? Are you alright?"

She hesitated and then I could see she made a deliberate decision to paper over the strange response.

"I'm fine. And no one knows anything, like I said." I knew I should've dug deeper, but I was too soft at that minute and decided to go down another road.

"Why would your sister volunteer to have pornographic photos taken of her?" Marie paused longer than she should have, but not long enough to indicate complete understanding of the situation. She inhaled another breath of smoke, but only to cover... something.

Before she could add more details, I heard a vibration emanate from my pants that were on the floor next to the bed. Twisting so I could remain close to her, I reached the pocket that housed my cellphone. I was just able to extract the phone when it vibrated a notification again.

She added from behind me: "Popular guy I guess."

My head was swimming from the previous exertion, but I could make out that there were in fact several new notifications that morning. I tapped and brought up a news item.

A certain Mathis Talbot had kicked the bucket, somewhere in the Hollywood Hills. It was a little sooner than I was expecting, but I wasn't shocked that he'd been found.

According to the bulletin, at some point during the previous night, Mr. Talbot had apparently been murdered in his own house. His gardener had seen the body through the front picture window and called it in. As it turned out, Mr. Talbot was, among other classless things, an 'amateur' pornography distributor and producer. The amateur bit of course implies nothing, as any yokel with a camera could pull off that gig; I would too if I was smart. Then I snapped out of it. All of a sudden even the presence of Marie couldn't quell the chill that slipped down my spine like an icy tentacle. I wished I could smoke just one cigarette at that very moment. The death of the tunic-wearing Mr. Talbot was about to throw me right into the middle of a murder investigation.

Out of silent desperation, I moved in to try to assess the condition of Ms. Upton's lips with my own, but she replaced the cigarette and wouldn't let it drop. I regained my composure.

I said: "I'll probably get a call soon asking me to come in for questioning. The man I found your sister with last night, the one who was shot, has just been discovered."

Her only response consisted of another inhalation of her cigarette and a pulling up of the sheets to cover her bare breasts. Needless to say, I got businesslike quick.

She only offered: "I'm sure you'll maintain any confidentiality that I'm owed, as your client."

Her frosty statement caught me out at bit, but I didn't have any great responses in reserve; my liquor and sex soaked brain had swelled beyond the scope of my skull by that point.

I did manage to find it a little odd that she didn't ask whether I had killed him. Maybe she didn't care, or didn't care to know herself. I tried to replicate my morning routine I maintained at home, but couldn't. I swayed out of Ms. Upton's bed courageously and managed to find my bunched up pants on the ground. I attempted to smooth out the wrinkles, gave up and started a limp search for my shirt. She watched with what can only be called disdain. Maybe I just didn't like her that minute.

I straightened myself out, struggled for words and failed. I leaned over the bed, and over her. She smoked like I wasn't there.

As she brought the cigarette up for another drag, I slapped her hand away. It was loud; a little too loud for a guy like me. Her bright blue eyes narrowed as she glared up at me.

She said: "I don't love you, so nothing to worry about, right?"

I didn't bother to respond to the cryptic statement, but instead bent down, grabbed her lower lip with both of mine, gave it a tug and smoothed her tongue out for her.

I replied in my most brazen tone, "I'll be in touch."

Without so much as a nuzzle I stood up and patted myself on the back for being the tough guy I was supposed to be. I made for the door, then turned to look back and survey the scene. Her left nipple unfairly peeked from behind the sheet.

10

I think sunsets are swell. They seem to imbue the viewer with a sense of accomplishment, that they finished another day on Earth. Sunrises are terrible.

The sun was as bright as ever, trying desperately to burn through the protective layer of haze that normally envelopes Los Angeles in the hours before 9 a.m. I plowed through what I perceived to be thick vapor, but I knew was actually just my muddy imagination.

I turned north onto La Brea and then onto Hollywood. Though I always thought it should be empty that early in the morning, there were a few stray tourists floating around on the sidewalk. I could never fathom how someone would go on vacation just to get up early, but I knew as usual I was probably in the minority. Before I started feeling too bad for myself, I tried to refocus. There wasn't a ton of time left to prepare for what was coming.

A slight murmur was all my car could muster, as I found my allotted spot back at my complex and stored her within. I gingerly helped myself out of the driver's seat and slowly made my way toward the elevator. There were so many variables to take into account in the developing case; it was a shame I wasn't very good at math.

The elevator made a distinctly virtual ding as I stepped aboard at about 6:14 a.m. After a forgetful transition into pajamas, I tumbled into bed around 6:30 a.m. I knew there wasn't a ton of time to regain my senses, so I tried to sleep, and failed. My mind roved.

The pornographer's death was going to be a pain to deal with, especially given that I was still working a case that may or may not be linked to the murder. The ballerina only offered herself as a consolation, which I had taken, and to be honest, enjoyed wholeheartedly. Mr. Costello had disappeared mysteriously as far as I was concerned, but I was fairly certain no one else was concerned about that particular fact, either. As for Stacy, it dawned on me she could be halfway to San Francisco by now, as I'd trustingly, and foolishly, left her alone the night before following her ordeal at Talbot's.

Then I moved onto more introspective thoughts, such as why I had gotten myself into such a cognitively eroding business such as this. Luckily, before I could delve too deep, I thought I might have glimpsed the Sandman in the far corner of my brain.

I had finally resolved to forget my troubles and shut myself down for a while when the house phone rang.

The phone displayed a downtown Los Angeles number. I answered it as I would any other possibly important call.

I offered: "Hello?"

I got: "Marsden. I don't have a ton to say. The assistant D.A. wants to see you. Come on down, by noon."

"I appreciate it."

"It's not a favor." Quinlin Halle had just offered me all he could, and it wasn't going to be nearly enough.

11

Noon approached faster than I would've liked. I only had time to shower and don a new outfit, then take the subway downtown at twenty minutes to noon.

The problem with the subway isn't the fact that it's below ground or noisy, but that all the clientele appear one hundred percent defeated by the society that put them there. If you want a dose of what it takes to live in a modern American city, take the subway. Having said that, if you want a dose of what it's like to die in an American city, take a bus.

I reached downtown a few minutes shy of my noon deadline and started my trek toward city hall. I'd gotten Quinlin involved, so the Hollywood substation was a bit inadequate for what I was into now.

A few birds chirped on the three trees between the subway stop and the iconic city hall. They seemed to want to warn me about what was going to happen, but they wouldn't be subject to certain reprisals if I failed to show. Damned birds.

As I arrived at the classic building, I opened my coat and took as deep a breath as I could of Los Angeles air. I choked only slightly as I entered the musty but lovingly restored lobby and headed for the elevator. The marble was just a bit too slick I thought, as I got into the brass-laden, ornate elevator car. Then I remembered my ideas stopped mattering the moment I set foot in this building. The district attorneys' offices were on the fifth floor.

I hit the appropriate button. Before the doors could close, a mousy brunette stumbled her way past the threshold. She had thick glasses and carried enough folders to populate at least one section of the Library of Congress, but I didn't feel it appropriate to offer my help. She was probably the enemy; I needed to get in the right mind-set.

She managed to nudge the third floor button and I managed a partial grin as she looked at me with critical, muddy brown eyes. She didn't realize it wasn't my fault that she had to carry all those folders.

Before I had a chance to give myself a final pep-talk, I arrived at floor number five and stepped out of the elevator into a nice but extraordinarily generic lobby. An auburn-haired receptionist sat behind a laminated wood desk in front of the wall I faced. She reminded me vaguely of a pigeon. She first eyed me with the right, then the left eye, before she went back to tapping on her keyboard. She obviously had a lot to do on her computer. I only merited a quick assessment. Before I could make any more judgments, I walked towards her. I hadn't said anything but she responded robotically anyway:

"Mr. Rodriguez is engaged until noon. Do you have an appointment?"

I managed a quick glimpse of my watch, which revealed it was unsurprisingly twelve-o-three.

I remembered I live in Hollywood and schedules are for suckers.

"I'm Duncan Marsden. I got a call from Quinlin-" was all I was able to manage before a flurry of keystrokes drowned out my words. I watched the bird's fingertips flutter across the keys. Then she paused and tapped a button on her office phone and said into her headset:

"I have Duncan Marsden for you. Yes sir." She tapped the button again and looked up at me. "Please wait for entry."

For some reason I'd had a shred of hope that the meeting would turn out to be a friendly chat. Her unwavering formality seemed like a bad omen.

I stood there and waited for what must have been almost thirty seconds before the door opened and I gingerly walked into a cave of an office.

Assistant district attorney Peter Rodriguez's office was darker and more upsetting than it should've been, given his rank and employment. Then I remembered the sorry state of the City's finances. Rodriguez sat behind a mass-produced mahogany desk that would've been stylish half a century earlier. It would've been delightfully retro, had it not been for its shabby, vulgar olive green finish, probably applied by some schmuck around 1977. No doubt a schmuck had thought he knew best; as I took a seat across from Rodriguez in a stiff wooden rolling chair I tried to reassure myself that I wasn't a schmuck, usually.

12

Peter Rodriguez was as solid as a man could be and still be a human made of flesh. While I'd heard about him and read a few excerpts from an interview with him in some lightweight magazine, I'd never actually met the man before. People had mentioned he did in fact possess integrity, and his ideas about improving the city's justice system had actually been lauded by both politicians and the public alike, which seemed to suggest he was a pretty smart guy. Now that I saw him in person, he vaguely reminded me of a dishearteningly grey, breathing bank safe. Taken all together, it meant that he'd be impossible to assuage with my own brand of flippant logic. This was going to be a long day, and probably night.

The man was about fifty-two years old, and had a grey slash on each temple against a full head of slicked back, jet-black hair. As I shifted in my chair, the only thing that moved were his granite-tinged eyes. The rest of him was perfectly still, save his right hand, which held a fancy burgundy ballpoint pen that wobbled, slightly and deliberately.

His office faced east; the worst for someone such as myself who favored progress over triviality. Just as I thought I had gotten a fair read on the situation, two shadows appeared from the darkened right rear corner of the room.

One of the newly discovered men had the sallow eyes I had come to associate with a Dickens novel. His waxy face didn't change as he emerged from the shadows. He was lanky, but appeared to have strength in his spindly appendages. I didn't doubt for a minute that he'd be trouble.

His apparent partner was shorter and uniquely pudgy. His playful red suspenders suggested he might not be the worst guy in the room. The problem was his face registered the type of muted disgust normally reserved for the discovery of a dead rat on the front lawn.

D.A. Rodriguez was an import from Chicago. More accurately, he had been born in LA but grew up in Chicago. He'd now returned to finish an impressive career. I knew he'd be polite, which was very nice. But I had a feeling he wasn't feeling generous given the way I had been invited down to "headquarters." I had a vague notion the Midwestern charm had been rubbed off completely by LA's glittering grit. Rodriguez took a puff of a decidedly illicit cigar. I decided not to remind him that smoking had been outlawed in public buildings for at least twenty-five years, and instead folded my hands neatly over my lap and braced for impact.

"Good morning Mr. Marsden." Rodriguez paused as he took a last puff of his cigar and then ground it into a discrete ashtray on the windowsill behind him. He seemed to take note of the sun, then corrected himself, politely of course.

"Excuse me, good afternoon. I've been filled in by Quinlin, but, well, I'm sure you can guess what I want now."

"The details," I offered.

"Exactly." He wanted to take another satisfying draw from his cigar, but he had already snubbed it. The circles under his eyes grew ever-so-slightly darker.

I said: "I'll tell you what I know, but it's not much. Plus I do have client confidentiality to keep in mind." I immediately wanted to slap myself, because I was setting myself up for a painful debut in custody.

"As you know there's no such thing as PI-client confidentiality. Having said that, I'm prepared to be pretty pragmatic about this whole thing, as you did report it on your own volition."

A voice from the corner interrupted: "I ain't."

The taller shadow with the sallow eyes didn't even seem to move his lips when he talked. He took a step forward and seemed to cringe when some light from the window fell across his face.

D.A. Rodriguez looked tired as he made the introductions: "Mr. Marsden, Detective Donnelly and his partner Detective-"

"You skipped us Marsden. The Talbot case is my case." Donnelly didn't seem to recognize the fact that the assistant district attorney theoretically outranked him, and that he had just interrupted him. I took that as a bad sign.

"I'll throw you in the tank without thinkin' twice. Just spill it." He sounded convincing, for a cartoon cop.

"I already offered to cooperate."

His blood refused to settle: "We all know that's a load. Mr. Rodriguez, sir, I would like a chance to question this 'ere witness myself."

The detective had a drawl that was not from California. He shouldn't have been allowed to wear a badge in the state with that accent. Then I got a hold of myself, since my brain was still pressing the inside of my skull from the night before.

Rodriguez even hesitated for effect, "Detective Donnelly, I want to give the man a chance to do the right thing here. And I want some good, honest testimony."

Donnelly didn't like it at all. He produced a tin of snuff that was also out of character for the region, pinched a bit and tucked it away carefully in his lip. The pudgy partner hadn't moved since I first noticed him; he still sat quietly in the shadows behind Donnelly.

I told the assistant D.A. my account of events, leaving out Marie where I could, trying to stick to the story of misappropriated talent for pornography involving a Stacy Upton. Rodriguez sat there and didn't even bother to take notes. I talked slowly enough to notice the beams made by the sun shift to my left and then fade completely.

The day was waning and I still wasn't in custody. That was something.

■ ■ ■

Throughout my story Donnelly glared unblinkingly. His eyes may have even gotten a bit red towards the end from a lack of blinking. He still wasn't impressed. The long sigh Rodriguez emitted at the end of my story signaled a similar sentiment. There were too many holes, and everyone knew it.

Then Rodriguez started his questioning: "Alright, so what motivated you to ram down this Talbot's door again?" He looked as though he was starting to tighten the noose.

"I heard a shot and figured I should intervene. As a concerned citizen, if nothing else."

Donnelly huffed loudly and drew a glance from Rodriguez, but it wasn't a scold. Rodriguez went on: "Alright, so you break down the door and find Talbot already shot. Where was the girl?"

"Stacy?" I was a little miffed he didn't even decide to use her name that I had anguished over divulging.

"Yes."

"She was," I took a breath to signal my obligatory distaste, "sitting on a faux-sarcophagus. Naked."

"Naked?"

So all the people in the room were still men. There was a longer than natural pause as they thoroughly imagined the important evidence I'd just revealed.

"Did she have any sort of firearm in her hand, or near her?"

"No. I already told you that the gunman must've run out the back. I heard him."

"You heard somethin'," Donnelly piped up, annoyed.

"I'm only telling you exactly what I found." I felt I was starting to run out of my cut-and-dry explanations, but they seemed to be tolerating it for the moment. "Could I get a water or something?" There weren't many things left to say and I wanted to milk them for all the hospitality I could before the inevitable.

Rodriguez ignored my request completely. I felt like I was a child pulling feebly at his pant leg, and he'd shaken me off.

"The girl had all the motive in the world, with him taking, let's say, questionable pictures of her, perhaps for payment or blackmail purposes. Why wouldn't she kill him?"

"She would," I admitted, "but she didn't. She may have chosen to be there all on her own. We really need to figure out why the pictures were taken in the first place."

Donnelly made another inordinately loud huff that threatened to disturb the papers on the assistant D.A.'s desk.

He said, "look Mr. Rodriguez. This guy is as honest as muffler dealer-"

As I was thinking about how folksy was too folksy, Rodriguez replied:

"Detective, I'm just trying to glean all the information I can. Mr. Marsden says he's being helpful. I'm taking him at his word at the moment. He theoretically has no reason to lie."

Donnelly added an unhelpful "That we know of."

The bickering fascinated me, as I always enjoyed watching one city employee harry another, but a heavy part of me knew while this might be entertaining, it wouldn't end up benefitting me. They weren't buying what I was selling, and I was running out of options.

13

Two hours later and we still all sat in roughly the same positions; although I had a feeling mine was the least comfortable of all. Donnelly had retreated back into the dark corner again, only coming forward to huff and puff at various things I said. Rodriguez still sat in his government-issue high-backed leather chair, barely engaging the tilting mechanism. The overly shiny red leather upholstery seemed to be aging and cracking before my eyes.

I continued to sit in a wooden chair that perhaps the local diocese had thrown out. As I pondered which of my vertebrae the slats of the chair were crushing, Rodriguez went about his work.

Every once in a while he would type something one-handed into his laptop and then ask an inane question about a certain detail I would of course know about. After a while he took a deep breath, made a final click of the mouse but didn't look up: "So you maintain that Stacy Upton had no role in the murder of Mathis Talbot?" It was a significant question delivered like an afterthought. He sounded about as interested in my answer as he would've been picking new drapes for his office.

"None whatsoever damn it." I was getting bored at this point too. The outside light was gone and so was any pretext of civility.

"Alright Mr. Marsden, I'm satisfied that you have coop-erated at least as much as is needed at the current time. I trust you not to leave town and use common sense however." It seemed he was looking at a blank wall as he addressed me.

"I'll do my best." I was being just a bit difficult. Rodriguez understood; the two cops definitely didn't.

Rodriguez was reasonable enough: "I'm releasing you on your own recognizance. I'm sure you won't be far if I need you. Have a nice evening Mr. Marsden." He exhaled, as though the ceiling might be resting on his compact, solid shoulders.

I stood up under the wary eyes of the two shadows in the corner. They had drifted into obscurity for the rest of the interrogation, but I swore I could hear them breathing down my neck the whole time.

I adjusted my coat and surveyed the scene.

Rodriguez sat there, struggling not to light another stogie in my presence. He appeared done for the day. The two shadows hovered anxiously. It seemed to me I didn't have a long walk ahead of me.

Before I could make any specific suppositions about what would happen next, I decided to turn and leave to try my luck. I twisted the nob on the old-fashioned office door and let myself out into the dim hallway.

As if on cue, I was immediately flanked by the two shadows. The door closed quietly behind them.

"You leave like you thought you'd be leavin'." Donnelly was distinctively unintelligent in his assessment of the situation. I already knew I'd gone too far before I spoke:

"You going to keep up with that ridiculous lingo all the way to the lobby or are you going to haul me in? You should decide before you do what you're gonna do." It was like I was drunk. It wasn't a wise idea to prod an angry, pseudo-bumpkin. I went on: "I've done nothing wrong and your boss let me go, let's call it a draw, and that's being generous."

Donnelly's nostrils flared more than they should've as he lunged for me: "he ain't *my* boss, wise guy."

Before I could comment on his iffy banter, he slammed me against the thin office wall of some lower level bureaucrat on the same hall as Rodriguez. Of course the A.D.A. couldn't hear such an obvious racket.

He had the cuffs on me, and tight, before I could catch my breath. He started: "Alright smart guy–"

"I take this to mean I'm in custody? What for?"

"Obstruction of justice. And I don't like your face."

"I'm not sure the latter one is a legitimate charge."

"O' course it is. Shut up."

His silent, pudgy partner grinned. The Golden Gate couldn't have spanned the gap in his two front teeth.

14

Located directly across the street from the city hall was the much newer and gleaming Police Administration Building. It looked as though a shiny, silver cube was being eaten by a grey trapezoid. The only thing that really struck me was how incongruous the aging Donnelly and Pudgy looked entering the place.

I squinted as we proceeded across the courtyard in front of the entrance. The late afternoon sun seemed to be glaring directly into my eyes off the building. The shot of sunlight afforded me an odd mental boost. Then we went inside and all my organs felt squished together.

It was the most sterile building I'd ever been in. Before I could marvel at the irony of who should inhabit such an apparently clean place, we took an elevator to a hallway, and at the end of the hallway, we entered an interview room right out of the movies.

There was a one-way mirror on one wall, a tiny exterior window protected by a new glazed-metal grille and a camera mounted in a high corner with a view of the whole room. I was standing, evaluating my surroundings, when Donnelly pushed me and I tumbled over the chair in front of me and onto my face. Before I could probe for any missing teeth with my tongue, Donnelly hoisted me back up and sat me down in an uncomfortable interrogation chair. I tasted a salty mix of saliva and blood.

"Whoa there pal, you gotta be careful in cuffs, you can't just put your hands out, ya know?"

As I sucked my torn cheek, I noticed it was just Donnelly and me in the room. Pudgy was missing.

"Alright, what do you want? You heard the story, I have nothing else to say." I knew it wouldn't make any difference, but I needed it on the record.

Donnelly appeared to weave a bit, then came down quick with his right and punched me in the neck. I tumbled off the chair and again found myself on the ground. The bleeding hadn't stopped.

"I'm not sure that kinda stuff is gonna hold up in court these days, Donnelly." I tried to motion toward the camera with my chin.

"Ha, 'member how city's in a budget shortfall? Camera's broke." My spirits really did sink then. "Do you act like a hick just to give yourself some leeway?"

He walked over to me, wound up and kicked me as square as he could in the stomach. I've been known to do some crunches in my time, but they didn't seem to figure in at that moment.

I sputtered and some of the blood and saliva mixture from my first wound came shooting out onto Donnelly's shoes. He looked annoyed but not surprised.

Once again he pulled me up by the left arm and sat me down. I took some deep breaths while I had the chance.

He said: "You know, I get you're one of these gritty PI types, but come on, I just want the simplest information and you won't give it." He gave a sideways glance at the mirror.

"What happens if I really was telling the truth to the A.D.A.?" It was worth a shot. Whatever the tough situation, I always gave Common Sense a chance to magically reveal himself and show my enemies the righteous way forward. He always seemed to stand me up.

"You weren't." He took a step toward me again and I tensed my core, but nothing happened. He stepped back again just as quickly and took a seat across from me. His waxy face still didn't move as he tried to size me up. I silently noted he was in fact correct about my facts being off; I had tried to bend the facts enough to simplify the situation without changing the results. I still didn't like him though.

"Look pal, I don't have a lot going for me these days, but I can still solve a homicide or two before they kick me out."

"Kick you out for what?"

"Being old."

"Well your partner looks old too."

"Naw, he's just fat." In another era he would've sparked a cigarette and maybe even offered one to me too. Instead he just took a disappointed breath and opened his eyes a millimeter wider. "I get you get how this works, but I'm just trying to cut through the crap, see?" He wiped his nose with his fingers and dropped his hand again. This guy was about done, not just with me, but with everything.

I tried some rationality: "If you think I know how it works, then you'll also know I'm not going to add to anything I said before." I was going to include a snide remark, but I started to feel a trickle of something liquid and warm drip down the right side of my face. As I hadn't been crying, I guessed it was more blood.

"Schucks." This guy was all nostalgia all the time. "I'm holdin' you anyway."

"For a crime?" I was ready to push my luck; I'd already written off the night anyway.

"Nope, as a material witness," he calmly replied.

"I'm pretty sure you're not allowed to do that."

"Well I guess we'll see, huh?"

"For how long?" But I knew I wouldn't get an answer. He was going to do what he could get away with.

Donnelly was one of the last ones who could pull off the real tough-cop persona. He didn't care about the consequences and he'd do what he said. I was in for at least a night. I was almost alright with it.

15

The contemporary jail cell is nowhere near as romantic as its historic counterpart. Probably due to my special "material witness" status, I was granted a private holding cell with eggshell colored walls and a barred, frosted window to the outside world. It would remind me whether it was day or night, and that I wasn't free. The classic prison bars have since been replaced with an uninspired reinforced steel door with a metal wire-reinforced window inset vertically. I had a thin, plasticky mattress and a metal toilet and sink combo unit, complete with a shined-metal mirror. This was pretty good, considering where I was. Most importantly though, I was alone.

Before I'd been shoved into my enclosure, I'd managed a glimpse of an analogue wall clock which indicated it was almost 9 p.m. The darkness outside my trusty frosted glass window seemed to confirm it. Just as I was getting settled, the lights snapped off without warning, so I fumbled my way over to the bed and laid down.

I was finally stretched out, and while there was a pain in my neck from a certain police detective, it was almost a satisfying pain. There are certain things a private dick has to endure, and then there are certain things a man has to endure. I was certain this experience was one of the two, but then something unexpected crept up and bit me: my mind.

It had finally ticked over to wide awake and was ready to process what had happened earlier in the day. I could feel a sweat start to emanate from my forehead. I had no sheets, and I was already too hot.

I was sacrificing myself for a reason, but it probably wasn't the right one. It wasn't for justice or the truth, but for the ballerina herself. This should've been a pretty straightforward case, at least I was sure that's what an uninformed outside observer would see. The assistant D.A. would be one of those observers, and that didn't bode well.

There were very few things I could put together about the case without a notepad, but I tried to order them in my head anyway. On the surface, someone was taking advantage of Stacy or blackmailing her by shooting illicit pictures of her. The ballerina seemed to be in the dark about it, and thus had hired me. Her husband was an unknown quantity. He didn't seem capable of shooting Talbot in cold blood just because his wife told him to for the sake of revenge, even if his ballerina wife was more alluring than the average wife. Then again, he didn't seem to bother with his wife much at all, which frustrated me more than anything, since I'd never ignore her if given the chance. I supposed I was still a reasonable suspect for the murder, although right now I had no more motive than anyone I could figure.

After a while I began to feel I'd been dropped in the middle of the Pacific Ocean, swimming in a direction only dictated by questionable thoughts. I had no encouraging landmarks. I was simply swimming on faith that at some point I'd hit land before I drowned, and that said land wouldn't be Antarctica.

My lids had finally started to descend due to a mix of confusion and exhaustion when the unforgiving fluorescent lights ominously buzzed on again. I opened my eyes and continued to lay there, not sure what to expect. The door opened with a wrenching iron groan.

"Well, well, and we don't even have any cigars." Quinlin Halle, stomach and all, stepped in. He was dressed to the nines and looked far too happy.

16

Quin managed a clichéd belt adjustment before he leaned against the shiny, eggshell-colored wall opposite the bunk I was laying on. I said:

"That's too bad, and here I thought there was no smoking in public buildings these days. But maybe people let things slide around here, huh?" The image of Rodriguez's slatey eyes cloaked in forbidden cigar smoke flashed through my brain.

Quin replied easily: "I know. It's one of the few failings of our fair city." If he'd had a cigar, he would've extinguished it dramatically. I probed my split lip and torn cheek with my tongue.

He noticed my injury and continued: "Ah, and sorry about that, but you know I can't step on too many toes; gotta keep some capital for when it matters. Donnelly's a bully, but at least he's still honest. Plus, I figured you could take a thump or two for old time's sake." Then he got to his real purpose. "So we know you didn't kill anyone, I just need a story for the D.A. so he can clear you."

The lip had apparently failed to teach me anything:

"You don't know that. Plus, I already told him a story."

"Well we have a hunch. Since you came down for the meeting, there's been another development that we feel is related." Quinlin smirked and clicked his teeth.

"Who's had it now?" I was legitimately flustered; I hadn't seen what was coming.

His weight shifted from one foot to the other and he slightly readjusted his stance against the wall. He was still the authority, but slightly less comfortable with the fact.

"It seems a Mr. Edmond Costello has been found dead under the Hollywood Sign in Beachwood Canyon." He took a deep breath and cracked a slightly-too-snazzy smile.

"That's a shame."

"I'm sure you're devastated." He didn't seem to breathe this time, but was still able to deliver another crooked but bleached smile. "As it turns out, you may just be in luck, since he was killed about six hours ago according to the powers at be. It seems you were in the custody of some rather hospitable detectives at the time."

I choked an audible acceptance of what he just said. It meant the ballerina was alone at the moment, too.

Without showing too much effort, I pulled my legs up, inhaled visibly, swiveled and threw my legs over the side of the bunk. Quin didn't move.

There weren't a ton of moves I could pull at that particular junction. I played it cool.

I said: "So you've done your act, what's the deal? I'm not the convict type and you know it, so why am I still here?" I had delivered my line with the right level of intention, but then again, this was Los Angeles… and it was a line.

"I don't think it'll be much longer, the D.A. just wants some closure as to what you know about Stacy."

"I told him what I know."

"There's more to this whole thing and you know it, Marsden. Spill it so I can spring you from this hole." He looked around disdainfully. It was pretty hokey.

"Just make sure they don't forget about me down here." I tried to flash one of my own distasteful smiles, but I think I just looked smug.

He exhaled in a very pronounced fashion and shrugged his shoulders too hard.

"Like I said, shouldn't be too much longer." He'd given it his best shot, but everyone knew I was a dead end, at least for the moment. He turned to leave, but shot a fairly benevolent grin at me before he stepped back outside.

Without turning back around, he offered one more tidbit:

"Most of Mr. Edmond Costello was found in some bushes right off the main trail by some very appalled joggers."

"Most?"

"He was missing his hands and feet, and head. DNA is the only way they even figured out who it was. He'd been pinched on some suspected kid-touching stuff at some school, but was never convicted. His DNA was still in the database of course. Gotta love that Supreme Court."

I knew Quin was waiting for a reaction, which I failed to deliver. He proceeded after he was convinced I had nothing to add: "The police are linking the Talbot murder to Edmond Costello's murder."

"Why? They're not connected, are they?" Dumb is always the way to go in a police station.

I quickly realized Quin had come here not just for duty, but out of curiosity. No one could legitimately connect the two murders, except through one person.

The ballerina was too good for it. She was too good for all of it.

Message delivered, Quin bid a hasty retreat. I didn't blame him. The mess of the ballerina and multiple homicides was becoming just a tad dramatic.

17

Anyone could've dismissed the Talbot murder as a deranged dancer out to avenge her vulnerable younger sister. And then, why not, might as well take care of a certain abusive husband too. The problem was, though he didn't deserve her, Mr. Costello wasn't capable of anything near violence, and thus wasn't worth murdering, at least due to domestic issues. That left a definite lack of motive. Over-parked cars during rush hour on a Tuesday were more blameworthy than Marie in my opinion. But it would need to be proven to all the authorities at this point, which would be an awful lot of work, and I still hadn't been paid for the last job.

A few hours later, the sunrise was the next light I was privy to. My train of thought drifted back to the enemy that is the sunrise, just as it had the day before. No West Coaster heralds the dawn as a new beginning; only the inevitable conclusion to a night that should've ended at least two hours earlier.

As I was cursing nature, metal clacked on metal. The cell door was being opened by a flatfoot I didn't know. Since they had let me keep my street-clothes, I didn't have much to do in the way of packing. I stood up, felt the welts from the night before, and walked out past the key-jockey. I didn't get very far.

"Good night?" It sounded like the only English he knew.

Standing behind the open cell door was Pudgy, Donnelly's previously silent, sweaty ball of a partner. He looked almost cheerful, like he was the eager maître d' at Musso's. Clearly he had spent his night on a slightly softer bed than mine.

"Bad night in fact."

He nodded slightly like he only partially understood: "Okay, let's go."

Without hesitation he spun around and started waddling down the hallway. I looked at the flatfoot, who was looking through me. I followed Pudgy.

We snaked through a maze of windowless corridors until we were back in the lobby atrium of the Police Administration Building. City officials and uniformed cops crisscrossed as they went about the morning business of policing. Then Donnelly popped out from behind a small potted palm tree. Pudgy retreated behind his partner and cracked his ridiculous grin.

"Enjoy your night in the can?" Donnelly's predictable repartee was simple, but still grinding for a guy who hadn't had the most restful night.

"Cleaner than my apartment."

"The D.A. thinks you ain't involved in any of the murders that I'm on now. You must have some sorta friend in there, huh? I ain't so sure."

"I'd be disappointed if you were."

"Cram it buddy, you ain't off the hook. Just for now." He stared into my eyes. I remembered I was pretty tired. I gave a counter stare and started to push past the duo. "You might not be good for Costello, but I'm not so sure about Talbot. And by the way, your girl is gone."

"My girl?" Donnelly must've noticed me go white, since he wasted no time. Fortunately, he wasted no time on the wrong girl.

"Stacy Costello is missing as of 5 a.m. this morning. No one knows where she is. Not even her sister. She's our lead, naturally, though the older one is on the radar too o'course."

"Oh, you have a motive then?" I wasn't even trying to be clever.

"We will."

I was going to add 'famous last words' before I caught myself and realized there was no reason for me to be there anymore.

I said: "Why are you telling me this?" It was like a movie, one of those fluffy, dramatic midnight runs on cable. I was almost having fun. Then my neck throbbed.

He looked like he had to go to the bathroom: "If you didn't kill Costello, one of them girls most likely did. I didn't tell you nothin' you didn't already know. Have a nice day." Without waiting for Pudgy, Donnelly sucked his gums and walked off. His partner gave another dumb smile and tottered after him.

18

As soon as I got out of the can and stepped out of doors into the undeniably agreeable sunny weather, I jumped in a taxi and didn't bother visiting the office. I beat it back to my apartment, took a long shower around 11:30 a.m., and tried to figure out the next move.

As I was drying myself after the shower, I called Marie. It rang at least three times before she picked up with her just-too-sultry voice:

"Duncan-"

"I believe you mean Mr. Marsden. I'm sure the police have contacted you by now. "

"Stop it…Mr. Marsden. They have contacted me-." All I could hear after that was apparently labored breathing and maybe a tear run down a cheek.

I wasn't in the fooling-around mood I guess:

"Meet me at the Luna Inn on La Brea at eight tonight. I could say more, but I'll say it then."

I knew I'd gone a little far with the patois, but I was only met with a dial tone. Nice work Marsden, this was going to be some date.

Maybe two seconds passed before someone knocked sharply. I gathered my towel and peeped through the hole. Quinlin stood outside looking impatient. I opened the door and he strode in unceremoniously. It wasn't surprising, and it wasn't exactly welcome either, but seeing as he was already in, I shut the door and offered him a drink.

He accepted and moved on to business:

"Up for a trip?" He swirled his drink and then took a long sip. He swished the alcohol around in his mouth before he swallowed with an audible gulp.

"At this point, should I care about the destination? Jail again maybe?"

"Relax Marsden. I think we should take a look at the Costello scene."

"That could seem like questionable judgment to some, since apparently I'm still a suspect for a murder." I was honestly a little concerned this time, though I knew I wouldn't pass up the chance.

"Only officially." He simultaneously finished his drink and raised his sleek eyebrows over the edge of the tumbler. A mischievous smile dripped off the glass.

I excused myself, went into the bedroom and quickly dressed in what I considered to be neutral clothes. There was a small mirror hung on the wall next to the bed. I examined my split lip from the night before. It almost looked like it was trying to heal. I reminded it not to get too comfortable.

I followed Quin out of my apartment and downstairs. He'd parked his large Jaguar sedan smack in front of my apartment. No one ever got that spot.

We motored over onto Franklin and headed east. I always considered it a version of traveling back in time, since the strip malls turned back into somewhat shabby but larger houses east of the freeway. These houses were built for the Hollywood big-timers quite a while back, when Hollywood was the only place to be. Now they were owned by yuppies with fancy cars, which they parked on the street. What self-respecting car owner who owns a perfectly good garage parks on the street? No one, that's who.

Before I could share my sour opinion with Quin, he took a sweeping left onto Beachwood and slipped along past some smaller, but still expensive, houses until we reached the extreme west end of Griffith Park. He slowed down only a little as the roadside dwellings became more obscured by foliage. Then it seemed we were just in the woods.

He piped up rather suddenly:

"You know, this place is usually only used by the mob for this kind of thing." I knew he wanted a conversation. I was tired, but still knew my place.

"You think they were in on it this time?"

"Well, I think whoever offed Costello knew what they were doing. From what I could see."

"You've already been here?"

"A friend sent over some photos. A dead body is almost never pretty. This one is especially ugly."

Quin lifted off the gas as we approached the more heavily wooded area with a sign that identified the entrance to the park. Eucalyptus mingled with oak as we silently floated through the base of the hills. Smells intermingled as well; eucalyptus with, well, dog shit it seemed. He pulled into a dirt parking lot ringed with police cruisers and a bunch of mingling patrolmen. We took a spot next to an unmarked detective's car and he cut the engine without ceremony.

With similar lack of ceremony, he produced a small handkerchief and dabbed his already glistening brow. He took the opportunity to bring me up to speed.

"He, or well, what's left, was found scattered around here."

"Scattered?"

"As in, bits and pieces."

"And I needed to see this in person?"

"Not needed, but I wanted you to. Might be helpful. We're still looking for parts of him." He neglected to mention for whom my presence would be helpful. I decided I could afford to pull the thread.

I said: "Why would they bother cutting off his hands and feet and then scatter them around the same area anyway? The mob usually only does that kind of job to hide an identity, and they're obviously smart enough to always get rid of the identifiable parts.

Quinlin only arched his eyebrows and smiled. "Maybe we're dealing with a wannabe, or a cheap hack." He tried not to look too pleased with his pun as he grasped the steering wheel and used it to haul himself out of the car. The suspension resettled and I opened my own door and stepped out.

It was pleasant enough in the shade, but I knew the sun would be beating down from its highest point once we left shelter. One of the many reasons I try to sleep past midday when I can.

Before I could ask more specific questions, Quinlin was already conversing with a plainclothesman standing guard at the entrance to the parking area. I could only hear murmurs, but I noticed a distinct lack of urgency among the cops assembled. I ambled over to the pair and immediately regretted it. The plainclothes cop silenced himself almost immediately and gave me a glare I estimated was normally reserved for teenagers driving while on their phones.

"It's alright Brisko, he's here with me."

The man who was apparently Brisko was still frozen when Quinlin decided to break us free.

"I'm taking him for a look, any new developments?"

"Nope." Brisko didn't thaw one bit, despite the climbing ambient temperature.

Quinlin only cracked a sarcastic smile, turned away from the sourpuss and led us down a hiking trail into the woods.

He was starting to pant as we passed the five-hundred yard mark. We weren't even in the sun yet.

"Still on that diet?" I added an appropriate snicker.

"You know, I still have this job for a reason," but he declined to say what it was.

We soon came upon two uniforms, a detective and a tech from what I gauged to be the medical examiner's office standing around a taped off area. Upon closer inspection, the uniforms and detective were struggling to avoid staring at a raggedly severed left hand and forearm partially obscured by a desert-type plant with long, pointy fronds. The tech didn't register the expected revulsion.

He said cheerfully: "Hey Quin, what'd I tell ya, he gave us a hand, right?" He opened his arms as if trying to frame the severed limb for a photo. It was very nice of the tech to lighten the mood given the circumstances. It also explained why Quinlin had such access to this particular crime scene. Quinlin had friends everywhere it seemed, and loyal to boot.

"That he did. Make sure to shake the other one for me, when you find it."

"Sure will."

"Make anything out of it yet?"

The tech took a moment to empty his lungs very slowly, then said: "Not much, but whoever did it was a pretty tidy fella. Looks like it was probably more about business than anger. No ancillary wounds or abrasions yet."

Quinlin turned to me and cracked a grin big enough to be seen from the Strip. I was only slightly impressed and slightly more interested. Then I felt just a bit queasy.

19

"The torso is already downtown, but they've been find-ing various parts of him since dawn." Quinlin again took what must've now been a very moist handkerchief and dabbed his brow. It was getting to be the afternoon, and quite hot. He seemed to shimmer at a slightly different frequency than the waves of heat emanating from the arid background.

I said: "So, why did you want me here?" It was an hon-est question that I knew wouldn't have a real answer.

"You're closer to this than everyone else, and while they don't really know it, I do. Call it a favor, for me."

I managed a slim smile but wondered what this was really going to cost me later. Then I looked at him again and he swayed a bit.

Without waiting for my larger companion, I wandered a bit off the trail and into the scrub. I'd always marveled at how a real, natural desert environment could coexist with one of the largest metropolitan areas in the world. While I'll still always marvel, that day my wonder was quickly squashed by a pulpy paper-weight.

"Quin. Get up here, I just did some more of your job for you." I wanted to sound in charge, but after the reality at my feet sank in, I immediately wanted to transfer responsibility.

Edmond Costello's head was carefully nestled under a low, dry bush. The plant was still a dull green color, despite the inexorable drought we'd been suffering the past few years. The dead man's eyes were a milky grey, which I could see clearly as they were wide open. Just like the other saw-jobs, it appeared to be a rough cut, this time at the neck. A dribble of blood from a bullet wound seeped from his right temple. His face looked pretty fake; he could've had a nice spot on Hollywood Boulevard modelling some less than enticing hats.

Then I noticed something that didn't quite fit the sweaty pallor of the rest of the head. A corner of some sort of white fabric slightly protruded from his mostly closed mouth. I was just able to make out a design of a lady bug on the fabric before Quinlin stomped up behind me.

"Oh ho, look at that. He doesn't look surprised to see you, I'll give him that."

It didn't seem appropriate, but even someone like Quin couldn't be expected to be reliably clever at one hundred percent of murder scenes.

Yet again he produced his handkerchief, acted out the requisite dabbing motions and leaned over the head, shading it from the sun.

"It's almost like he's sweating, eh?" He chuckled a bit, just enough to expose how nervous he really was. "What's that though? In his mouth." Of course he'd seen the fabric too. I wanted to manage the situation but knew who I was dealing with.

Without hesitation he carefully jerked the corner and teased out more of the ladybug pattern.

"Well, I should've guessed!"

Before long Quinlin had produced almost an entire pair of what would've normally been regarded as very adorable women's panties. Only a corner remained in Costello's mouth.

"I'm sure the M.E. won't mind your independent examination."

"Shut up Marsden, we both know what this is. The question is, which one was it?"

He meant which sister had brutally murdered and dismembered a corpse. I knew the answer was neither, but that meant exactly nothing since I had no idea who did. Before I could respond with a well thought out analysis, we were interrupted by the tech we chatted with upon arrival.

"Quinlin! What gives??" He rushed up and attempted to push Quinlin out of the way, though Quinlin weighed almost two hundred forty pounds, and the tech would've been lucky to have broken one forty.

Quinlin roared: "Kid! Get the hell back, this is evidence!"

I stifled a laugh as Quin finally took a small step away from the severed head. The tech moved in on his territory like a threatened blue jay. It was time to leave anyway; I had a date after all.

20

Quin got one of the uniforms to drive me back into Hollywood. The guy didn't seem to mind, since it was probably better than standing in the sun the rest of the day. Regardless, we both stayed silent until I remembered I hadn't checked my professional mailbox in over a week. I directed the officer to a restored building just across the street from the very elegant main Hollywood post office.

Shortly after starting in the private detecting business, I'd decided I needed a place to separate my professional life from the rest of my life. I didn't recognize that the two would essentially meld together, but it still was nice to have a place to drink that wasn't my apartment. Having said that, I found the rents in the supposedly downtrodden core of Hollywood to be awfully high, so I worked a deal to share an office with a small time modeling agent I'd met through an old case.

I got out of the squad car and without so much as a wave the officer drove away. I quickly jaywalked and used my combination on the number pad at the front door of the building. The doors clicked open and I walked into the under-decorated lobby. According to the management, the lobby was said to be "newly refurbished and very inviting." To some perhaps stained yellow linoleum was inviting, but I didn't count myself among that group. To bolster the swanky design, the management had also provided several knock-off sleek, modern-type chairs and a small table with a selection of dull magazines, including what seemed like a perpetually three-month-old copy of the *Hollywood Reporter*.

I reached the creaky but still regal wooden stairs and climbed to the second floor. Mothballs always came to mind in the hallway, and I always semi-consciously tried to hold my breath from the top of the stairs down the hall to my office. I'd always wondered what all the "models" who came through here felt when they sniffed the place. Always smelled like the slow slide into oblivion to me.

Three doors down on the left was a door with two name placards. The top one read "Arnold Segram, Segram's Artists" and the bottom one read "Duncan Marsden." It theoretically wasn't an official tenant deal, so I had tried to keep it simple.

After putting an ear to the door and hearing nothing, I knocked a few times as I simultaneously took out my key and unlocked the door. It opened into a small waiting room with another set of lackluster furniture and tattered magazines. It had one window that was cracked open about an inch and looked out onto the street. I remembered Arnold telling me it would get stuffy in there without the window open but with it open, all the added noise would make his already anxious clients more anxious. I didn't talk to Arnold much.

I walked over to the door on the left-hand side of the waiting room and opened it. When he rented it to me, Arnold had said he had used it for a meeting and private casting room. Without asking what that meant, I said it would be fine and moved my stuff right in. In this case, my stuff was an old, but solid wood desk, a few chairs for the clients and a padded chair for me. I tried to decorate the place once with some posters, but the result looked like an eleven-year-old's bedroom, so I'd taken most of them down again. The only one left was a contemporary abstract print that was so generic, no one could ever be offended by it.

Before I made it a foot inside, I noticed a pile of mail on the ground that had been very nicely slipped under my door. I had my pick of any number of credit cards and mortuaries it seemed. I tossed the mail in the recycle bin, shut the door and collapsed into my cushy chair. True, some of the stuffing was threatening to fall out, but it did tilt, so that was something. I already knew what I was going to do next, so I went ahead and did it. I pulled the office bottle out of the bottom drawer along with a short glass and slapped a very healthy slug of bourbon into it. Without a second thought I killed it and waited for a certain amount of calm to descend over me.

I put my dusty shoes up on the desk and tried to remember why I paid for the dump at all, before I realized that it was in fact quite stuffy in there. I went over to the window and opened it all the way. Immediately I felt a warm breeze flood into room and mix with the stale air. Before I could turn back around I heard a knock on the frosted glass inset of the exterior door, which was unexpected.

With a certain amount of trepidation, probably fueled by a combination of my recent, albeit brief, incarceration and the fact that I'd observed a disembodied head about an hour earlier, I went over and opened the door.

The woman couldn't have been more matronly if she had been wearing Queen Elizabeth's Crown Jewels around her neck. Before she said anything, she looked me up and down slowly. I returned the favor. She was a woman I gauged to be in her mid-sixties. Her hair was not so much styled as pruned, and very up, as opposed to down. She had delicate features that would've been pretty thirty years before, and now only echoed a lost, presumably better time. I didn't think pearls were in style, but they had been at one point in the past, so she was damned if she wasn't going to wear them. The rest of her seemed average enough, although for a woman her age, she still wore a fairly stylish skirt that ended right after the knees. Then my eyes went back to hers and I got the gist of the visit; I'd seen those eyes before.

She started cautiously: "Are you Mr. Duncan Marsden?"

I opted to play it cool and conservative, at least at first: "As a matter of fact I am. And you are Ms.-"

"Mrs. Claire Upton. Do you mind if I come in? I have an important matter to discuss."

I stepped aside and gestured to one of the client chairs. I shut the door and went back around to my own chair. She had already placed her very high-end handbag on my desk and sat quietly, her hands in a knot on her lap.

I started: "Well Mrs. Upton, I could guess why you're here, or you could start, if you like."

She didn't seem to like the tone I had struck, but she had clearly found it important enough to find me, so I figured there wasn't a ton I could do wrong at the moment. She shifted a bit, cleared her throat and sat there. Finally, she said:

"My daughter mentioned you in passing a few days ago on the phone and I wanted to meet you myself, as all this has gotten pretty terrible."

"What's gotten so terrible?" The bourbon was hitting alright, and I was feeling playful, but there was something amiss too.

"Well my daughter's husband of course!"

"Your daughter is Ms.-"

"Mrs. Marie Costello! I'm starting to wonder if I'm in the right place." Her unprovoked indignation was just a little over the top.

"I assure you you're in the right place. I've been involved in Marie's case from the beginning, unfortunately."

"Simply terrible business. I'm worried about her quite a lot now." She was urging me into her world, and I was about to oblige. I figured I should probably play along to find out what her visit was actually about. "What's wrong with Mr. Costello? I saw him just the other day; he seemed fine enough to me."

"Oh but he's…dead." It was a bad acting job. She attempted to look distraught, but this was Hollywood, and she was dealing with a professional.

"Oh, I'm sorry to hear that, I didn't know. What happened?"

This took her by surprise. Maybe she didn't think she'd have to explain the gory end of Mr. Costello. This was a high class lady after all. But I couldn't shake the feeling she was trying to stick to a script.

"Perhaps I should introduce myself more fully, I think I've gotten a little out ahead here. I'm Marie Costello's and Stacy Upton's mother; I just flew in from Bridgeport, and I'm very worried that my daughters could be in danger."

"Well that's slightly more helpful," I tried to add a chipper little chuckle but it probably just came off as more nonsense. "How did you know where to find me?"

"Well Marie of course. She mentioned that she had hired a man to look after Stacy, and I guess that man is you. And since Stacy is missing and now my daughter's husband has been…murdered, I decided I better fly out here and try to help. I was hoping you might have some idea where Stacy is, the police certainly don't. Do you think Stacy and the murder could be related?" There was that false urgency again. I desperately wanted another shot to cut through the morass this woman had brought in with her, but I strived to remain as professional as possible. I could do my poor, dreary little office that justice at least.

"The police have said there might be a relationship. I'm not so sure myself." With my ploy of enthusiastic ignorance floated, I paused and waited for the next salvo. I had a feeling her concern was extremely fake; it seemed likely that she was just crudely fishing for information. Luckily, I wasn't a fish of any kind.

She got slightly testier: "Look Mr. Marsden, I don't really know what your part in all this is anymore; I'm just trying to find Stacy and look after Marie. There has been an awful lot of death around both of them and I'm worried. It seems like the police out here aren't doing much of anything!"

"What do you mean out here?"

"Well, out here in California of course."

"Do you think they would do it differently in Connecticut?"

"Well of course! For one, we're the Uptons, so that wouldn't even be a question–"

"What does being an Upton mean exactly?"

She paused and turned a very hazy shade of crimson almost immediately.

"I think you're not taking me very seriously Mr. Marsden. I came here as a parent in need– "

"No, you came here trying to figure out exactly what's going on. I have a feeling you haven't even spoken to Stacy in ages." I waited for that one to land and blow the bridge. It didn't take, oddly.

Her voice immediately dropped and took on a rusty quality as she continued: "Look Mr. Marsden, like I said,

I don't know what your role is, but where I'm from, we respect a family's heritage and I'd expect the same amount of deference from you, if you even are a private investigator, or whatever you're called these days."

For some reason, my patience was running thin enough that it decided to pack itself up then and there.

"Mrs. Upton, is your husband here with you?" I wasn't sure why I asked about him directly; maybe it was some left over suspicion from questioning the ballerina, but it tripped her up just like it had tripped up her daughter, so I knew I was on to something.

"Daniel is… did not accompany me. He had to stay in Connecticut." She blinked a few times as if to fan the flames of the brilliant cover job she just lit up. I opted to blow them out. You don't need a fire in Los Angeles anyway, the temperature is always just fine.

"Mrs. Upton, you do realize just because you're from an old and no doubt very distinguished family Back East, you will get no special treatment out here. It's the reason you people never decided to move to California in the first place. Where's your husband?" I was shooting from the hip and I didn't care who or what I hit. I wasn't completely sure what had incited my entertaining new behavior, but people say alcohol does drive creativity.

She didn't respond right away, as she was stifling a certain amount of hyperventilation, but I knew I'd hit something juicy. She finally said, hoarsely: "I already told you he's not with me. If you don't know where Stacy is, I'm not sure I need to talk to you anymore."

"I'm almost positive you should, Mrs. Upton. It sounds like you have yet another family member that may be missing." I smiled and just may have gotten slightly more out of it than she did.

"Of course not!"

"What does he look like?" Something was starting to spark up in the back of my brain and I had a feeling I was closing in on what it was.

"Well, why should I tell you!?"

"Why don't we look him up, I'm sure you important types are on the internet somewhere." Before she could protest, I'd typed in Mr. Daniel Upton's name into my ancient laptop and the first image that popped up almost made my eyes fall right out of my skull. I'd seen that very same face in the coffee shop arguing with Mr. Costello the day before. Despite my private detective job status, even I had to admit, at times, the internet could be awfully helpful.

Before I could add any pithy remarks, she snatched her bag off my desk and stormed out of my office in a cloud of angst. I opted not to tell her something had slipped from her bag onto the carpet under her chair: A keycard from the Roosevelt Hotel.

Mrs. Upton would never give away the real reason for her visit, but her presence alone meant something. For some reason I got the feeling she legitimately didn't know of her husband's whereabouts. But I was willing to bet her trip to California was more than just to check in on the family. It seemed to me it might just be a good idea to figure out the connection... and the real location of her husband.

21

After the perplexing meeting with Mrs. Upton, I realized I'd better beat it, as my date with the ballerina was fast approaching. I only dropped by my place for a few minutes to settle my nerves. I resolved to not reveal that Marie's mother had paid me a visit. I consumed half a highball and a few spurts of eau du toilette before checking in the bathroom mirror. I wasn't displeased, but I didn't really know what I wanted from myself that night, let alone from Marie.

Like so many times before, I headed down to the garage and retrieved my trusty partner. I decided on the scenic route. The course I chose demanded I motor directly through Hollywood down the boulevard past several iconic landmarks and catch a left on La Brea. There's a time for sentimentality, and this was as good as any.

Having said that, La Brea is actually pretty boring below Santa Monica Boulevard; a whole bunch of fancy clothing shops and fancier furniture stores that are always noticeably devoid of customers.

The desolate geography was the perfect complement to my overly active imagination. I wasn't really sure what I was going to say to the ballerina. Those eyes were whirlpools for substantive thoughts.

Before I could question my own motives any further, I arrived across the street from the bar and easily found parking in front of a lounge-chair emporium. Emporiums don't exist anymore. I supposed that's why it was so easy to park.

I coolly exited my car and jogged across the street in between some lazily drifting traffic. The Luna Inn was located in an exquisite antique building surrounded by the detritus of late mid-century LA. I tried to focus on the brilliant art deco design and quell my emotions.

Beyond the façade, the entrance was actually quite modest. Mrs. Costello was not. She was wearing a satiny, backless black dress that stopped just above the knees. Her heels may have been an inch or two tall for the venue, but no one was kicking her out. The fabric hugged her consummately-shaped hips and tapered to the portion which covered her thighs. It clearly was an appropriate outfit for a widow.

I put on my most conciliatory face and grabbed myself a high chair next to her. She stared at me, smiling weakly with her pillowy lips. I didn't have the lips, but I shot back a comparable stare. It occurred to me that every single time I saw her, my heart bobbed up and down in my chest like an eager little ship being tossed around on the towering waves of a storm. I couldn't control it, and I supposed I wasn't meant to.

"Well, how about a drink?" There were very few ways to start this conversation, and alcohol seemed like a strong choice.

I ordered a martini stirred with a twist; she ordered a martini stirred with olives. My heart jumped just a bit. Breathing was a good thing, at least for the moment. No one likes to kid themselves. She said: "So, why did you want to see me?" She seemed a bit too jovial for a woman who'd just lost her husband. I wasn't sure how happy this should make me. I clearly needed my drink as quickly as possible.

"Fishing for a compliment?"

She didn't respond favorably, which I half expected. Thankfully our drinks had materialized.

"I'm not sure I like that question." She paused to take a gentle sip of her martini. "You said you had something important to tell me. So tell it."

I always liked a woman who could drink a martini with a straight face, and one who could hold her liquor *almost* as well as me.

"We found a portion of your husband today." I took a sip which indicated just a bit too much satisfaction for her taste, apparently.

"Awful." She turned forward and slurped her own drink. She finally looked pretty distraught. It was a play, a certain dark part of my mind hoped.

"Sorry to be graphic, but it's the reality. I thought they told you about the circumstances of his death…"

"They did, I just didn't want to re-experience them if I could avoid it." She turned with a candor I'd dreamt of. I sensed she was truly upset, perhaps even upset enough to re-orient her life. Maybe she was free.

"A pair of women's panties were found stuffed in his mouth."

"Duncan, really!" The indignation was real and I tasted bitterness, though there were no bitters in my drink. "What did they look like?" I was surprised she asked; I could tell she already knew the answer.

"White with little ladybugs on them." I took a gulp to back up my position. She wasn't impressed.

"They're probably mine, of course." There was a certain amount of resignation about her, but she didn't seem afraid either. "I also have no idea how they ended up there obviously. I didn't kill him. I really did love him, but you know that." I had known that, but I'd tried to forget it.

She started breaking down the cocktail stick that had secured her olives. It turned into a small pile of split lumber as we continued. I wasn't sure if she was trying to disarm me or soothe herself. Her complexion seemed to decay the longer we sat there. I took a long drink until the alcohol started to burn my esophagus. Then I took a leap, and I hoped I wouldn't land on her: "What does your father think about all this?"

Her eyes darted up like they'd been magnetized as her fingers stopped working the cocktail stick. We were both aware that I had just seen this, so she had to say something.

"Why do you want to know that? Why does he matter?"

Even she could see she was being overly defensive. I decided to put my cards on the table after all: "Your mother stopped by today, and she had more or less the same reaction. I'm starting to think there might be something to it."

"My mother? Here?" It seemed to be genuine surprise.

"Did you not expect her to get a little worried when your sister went missing and now your husband is dead?" I watched as her glorious facial features turned to stone in a second flat. "You know I'm going to look into it now. There's too much pointing to him being a player in all this, so you might as well give me the scoop on him, because it's going to come out one way or the other."

"Please, Mr- Duncan, please don't. He doesn't matter. Not anymore."

"Stop. You can't keep up the cryptic bit and assume I'll just go away. At this point I'm in this one pretty deep myself. You can help me or not, but this is serious. And you know it."

All she could do was give me a big glistening stare, and then she was on my shoulder, tucking her chin as deeply into the crook of my neck as she could. I knew I wasn't going to make any more progress with her, and I wasn't sure what else she had to offer. I felt a warm dampness form and knew it was tears. She just kept struggling to repeat something she'd probably said too many times in the past for it to be cathartic now: "I escaped, this was supposed to be it. This was it…" And that's all she could offer.

We bid goodbye stoically outside the Luna Inn after I settled the check. She kissed me on the cheek and I kissed her back the same way. The valet saw the whole thing, which is how I planned it, just to make sure I had an alibi in case something happened, but I wished it didn't need to be that way. He called her a cab and I waited until it arrived. I helped her in and she looked up at me with a closed-mouth smile and those iridescent blue eyes. I knew that look would sit in my skull for a few years at least. Before she could say anything else I shut the door and theatrically banged on the roof of the taxi. It sped away before I was done reminiscing.

22

Technically Stacy's apartment was still sealed. While I was briefly incarcerated, the police had discovered that she wasn't there, and sat on the place for a bit until they figured out she probably wouldn't come back. This was all according to Quinlin of course. The police are busy people; there are crimes to prevent and villains to thwart.

After the meeting with Marie, I'd finally been allowed to hit the hay for a solid seven hours. I arrived at Stacy's a little before dark the next day, thinking I'd just tinker my way inside. Outside her door I looked at the partially corroded lock. It would take some time but looked pickable. Luckily a slightly easier way in soon made itself readily apparent. A cold, cutting voice came without warning over my shoulder:

"Hey, buddy, what the hell you think you're doin'?"

I turned to find a bow-legged man at least twenty years older than myself, judging from the deep lateral ravines on his forehead. He wore a clean-ish white tank top, some jeans and a pair of ratty sandals more appropriate for teenage beach go-ers. Such footwear on such an individual was one of the few downsides of Southern California I supposed. His eyebrows were a bushy brown hedge and he probably had shaved that morning, but needed to shave at least two more times to get the desired effect. The cigarette that dangled from his lips didn't even appear to be lit. He removed it to address me:

"Who are you? Another cop? I'm done with you peo-ple. I did everything you people asked, Jesus." He replaced the cigarette, but as it wasn't lit, he didn't inhale anything.

"Are you the landlord?"

"Of course I'm the damned landlord. What the hell do you want?"

"Did you see when Stacy Upton left?"

He removed the cigarette and rolled it between his right thumb and index finger. I guess it was his version of sizing me up. It was more accurate than I was anticipating.

"Hey, you're a private eye aren't ya?" He smiled enough to give himself satisfaction.

"Yes. Hired by her sister. Name's Marsden, Duncan Marsden."

"To figure out where she went eh?" I could tell he was getting some pleasure from besting someone cognitively. I indulged him.

"Right again. Can you let me in?"

"The cops say no, but it's my building. Name's Slocum." He didn't add whether it was his first or last name just like he didn't make any moves to help me inside or shake my hand, but he didn't get angry either. "In New Jersey this'd never hap-pen. The cops there know people have things to deal with."

I wasn't quite sure what he meant, but having been to New Jersey very briefly, I was positive I didn't care.

"The older sister really just wants her found; she could be in danger."

"Definitely could be, buddy." He appeared to plant himself more firmly in the hall.

"Why don't we discuss this over a drink?" It was shot in the dark, but I had a good feeling.

"Oh, you got something?" His eyes opened wide for a split second. My inkling was correct.

"Of course, let me just go to my car."

"I'm in 107, buddy." He just stood there. I turned and left without him moving an inch.

Once outside the building again, I ran as fast as I dared to the closest big avenue, which happened to have a conveniently located liquor store. I bought a pint of rye. Rye works for both amateur and professional drinkers. If they're a fake, they drink it because they don't really know what it is and want to avoid embarrassment. If they're a professional, they just drink it. I hustled back to Stacy's building and headed directly for number 107. He opened the door without me even knocking; a professional.

It may've been his building, but he decided to fill it with very little of his furniture. The living room had a crumbling table meant for a patio with its two associated chairs situated in one corner. Opposite was a tube-based TV that was old enough to earn a second glance. Slocum produced two scummy glasses that he assured me were clean. Luckily we were drinking alcohol out of them.

I poured a slug in each glass and took a seat. Before he even touched his chair he'd downed the apportionment. I poured another and settled in for an agonizing chat.

"So you're private eh? Didn't get the memo there's an internet now for that stuff eh?" I let it ride.

"I mean, what can people like you guys get done these days? People can just internet that stuff!" He placed his empty glass back on the table and his pinky twitched expectantly. I gave him another pour. Taking advantage of opportunistic alcoholics isn't necessarily my style, but it's too easy to simply avoid. I needed to move forward.

After another twenty minutes of trivial exchanges, I convinced him to open Stacy's apartment, just for a few minutes.

"I get ya, buddy." He finally stood up and wobbled a bit while simultaneously scrounging his pockets for something. I assumed it was a key and I was right. I guessed he'd separated it from his main key ring, probably for the police.

"You know those coppers said this was still an active crime scene. I said it was my room and I intended to rent it if she didn't come back." He had to tell someone he had some ideas of his own.

After polishing off three quarters of the rye on his own, he led me back to Stacy's and unlocked the corroded dead-bolt. I hastily stepped in and he stood in the doorway behind me, quiet.

"So I guess, what, you want me to leave?"

I produced the remaining rye from my pocket and slung it at him. He moved too quick not to expect it and disappeared just as quickly.

23

The apartment was what any single girl living alone in Los Angeles would vehemently choose to live in. It'd been built probably in the 1920's and updated in the 60's. There was a generic flat-panel television perched on a disposable piece of furniture in the living room. A pale blue, faux-leather couch sat in front of it, with a few mass-produced bent-metal sculptures hanging on the wall above it. There was an air-conditioning wall unit; it didn't look worn out. Girls like Stacy never seem to get too hot.

The living room had been turned upside down. Bits of paper and other useless baubles were scattered everywhere. I knew the police had a warrant, but this wasn't the official style. Maybe someone else had bid Mr. Slocum a visit; it'd been too easy for me after all. Then again, laziness on the part of Donnelly could always be a factor.

I moved into the kitchen, which is what I'd consider to be hopeless. Besides some dilapidated cabinets and drawers, it had an oven, an ancient microwave, and a refrigerator that screamed do-not-open. I noted there was no dishwasher. Some think it's a luxury apparently; then I thought of Stacy washing her own dishes and couldn't picture it at all.

Next up was the bedroom. It was neatly adorned, though there seemed to be clothing strewn on every flat surface. I had a feeling that said articles weren't actually ransacked, but simply left by Stacy, and felt a bit better about the state of my own apartment; then I noticed an all French historical print of a *The Rules of the Game* poster, and felt certain Stacy didn't know French.

Despite the apparent vandalism in the living room, nothing in any of the subsequent rooms felt out of place or suspicious. I was beginning to think I'd just wasted $10.69 worth of alcohol when I opened up the bathroom.

There was the standard collection of perfumes and bath related products, and then there was a plastic thing that didn't belong. Its black matte body stood out from the assemblage of pink and off-white bath items surrounding it on the edge of the tub. A man's razor, right next to a pink female equivalent. I nudged the shower curtain a few more inches and uncovered a distinctly masculine can of shaving cream to accompany it. I opted not to touch it, knowing what manscaping it could be used for, but I had at least one small lead to go on.

Closing the door quietly behind me, I exited the apartment and promptly ran into a now pretty tuned up Slocum.

"Find what you were lookin' fer?" He struggled to keep his eyes open long enough to hear the answer.

"Nope. Did she live here with anyone?"

"Hell no, that costs extra buddy. She did have this big guy come around sometimes though. Built like a Buick. I was gonna kick him out once, but I thought it'd be bad for business." Or Slocum's face, I surmised. I ignored that Buicks were no longer a measure of quality or quantity.

"Know who he was?"

"Nope, but he wore a nametag. Course' I don't remember what was on it, but I saw it."

"I'm sure you did." I didn't think he'd pick up on the sarcasm. I was right.

"All I know is he walked here. Cause' he walked away."

"Could've parked around the corner."

Slocum was vexed by my response. He was sure that the mysterious man had walked, but he didn't know why or how to convey the fact. His watery eyes just stared again. I opted to take the exit.

It was all residential for at least four blocks in every direction except one. I'd finished what I came to do, so I decided to risk the fifteen minutes and take a gamble on the one direction that had promise.

Two blocks north and I was on Santa Monica Boulevard. It was dead. Even the liquor store I had visited earlier was closed. A sushi joint had just unplugged the neon "open" sign and the employees were trying to make the place presentable again. There was a closed cobbler's shop, an equally closed trendy pawn shop, a place that sold male spandex fitness attire and a very run-of-the-mill motor hotel.

I say hotel, but it was of course a motel. In all my years in Los Angeles, I'd never figured out how such places stayed in business. There's probably one motel for every square mile of city, and it was a big city. It didn't seem like there could be that many prostitutes or naïve, middle-American tourists. But who was I to ask how they stayed in business; I also guessed they all had better cash flow than I did.

As it was the only place that was even remotely open, I strolled toward the motel and tried to figure out what I was getting into.

Most of the windows were dark in the two story L-shaped complex. The office in the front was lit, the venetian blinds were down, but not closed. There was some movement, so I headed towards it.

I opened the door, which dinged in a very traditional way. Lo and behold, there was a small brass bell fastened to the top of the doorframe. As I was staring in awe at this sentimentality, I neglected to pay attention to the fellow manning the desk. He should've been very hard to miss.

I just caught sight of his "Tray" nametag when I realized he was the size of a refrigerator. Tray was built like a linebacker, but didn't have any of the scars of sport. His hair was neatly coifed and his jaw could've cut diamond. I quickly decided I wouldn't want to be on the wrong side of his pineapple-sized fists.

Before I got too far into sizing him up, I noticed he looked pretty unhappy that a customer had just walked in, which was strange considering the place was probably empty. Or almost empty, I hoped.

"Hi sir, sorry, it's pretty late, we're full up."

I responded: "No you aren't." His tactic to get rid of me was as quant as it was moronic. "It's not that late."

He said: "Sorry sir, we are, but I might have something." He quickly started typing something into a primitive computer. He clacked the keys with the urgency of a court stenographer.

As he was occupied, I dug around for my P.I. license and made to present it. He looked up just as I got it out. He paused for too long while he tried to figure out what the shiny thing in front of him represented.

I said: "Frankly sir, I'm a Private Investigator. I'm here about one of your guests." The official line still works on some schmucks.

"Oh, um, well, I'm sorry sir, but I can't give you any information about any of the people staying here." Those would be guests.

I was not pleased: "I sure hope I don't have to give the West Hollywood Sheriff a call, they're pretty tough on guys like you."

He couldn't have gone whiter if he was one hundred percent bleached Egyptian cotton.

"Mister, I'm sure you don't havta do that. I just can't tell you any specifics, my boss told me not to. It's not good business."

At least in movies most of the suspects are clever and have a plan in mind to foil a would-be aggressor. Tray was clearly a more simplistic breed. He had nothing and he gave me nothing. He was such a nothing that I couldn't directly crack him. I longed for the predictable incompetence of Slocum. My patience was wearing just a tad.

"Alright, fair enough. I understand. Just tell me this, do you have anyone named Stacy Upton staying here? She's a younger girl, slender, pretty."

He pulled his sheet impression again and I got slightly more positive.

"Ah, well, no, I don't think we do. Just a couple from Kansas and some sort of boys sports team."

"So you do have some extra rooms?" Even I get to have fun every once in a while.

"Um, actually, no, we don't, all full up."

"Ah, I see. Well I suppose I'll try down the street. Thanks all the same." It was too neat, which is just what he needed.

Hunches are what detectives rely on. Even with the advent of the internet and cellphones and everything else, there's a certain amount of insight only a bundle of neurons can provide. The brain has a way of acting like a dowsing rod for beneficial deposits of information scattered among a sea of useless thoughts. I still haven't found a computer that can do it, and I'm not even a crotchety ninety-year-old most of the time.

I stepped outside, and the bell jingled reassuringly behind me. Before I had even cleared the property line, the neon sign out front went off and the light in the office dimmed. Someone had just adjusted the blinds.

Silently I maneuvered around the corner of the office so I could observe the back exit, which opened quickly as Tray made his way out without looking around. He headed immediately up the stairs and down three rooms, before he knocked and a door opened. Before the door shut I was on the stairs and identified the room as 203. There was a light on, but the curtains were mostly drawn. Some shadows interrupted the thin sliver of light cast through the gap in the curtains. I decided to wait one door down for a while to see what developed, since I resolved that I didn't want to get into a fight with a sizeable, stupid bulldozer that evening.

After about ten minutes, the shadows didn't seem to be slowing down. In fact, some of them seemed more agitated than ever. Then I heard a crash.

I slid over to the shabby door handle, turned and pushed all in one motion. That's the problem with motor hotels. No security.

24

What I found wasn't surprising, but I was still in a danger-
ous spot. As the door swung open, I saw Tray between
the two queen beds, arms in front of his face. He peeked
through them at me tentatively. I promptly moved my attention to Stacy. She was in black brief-style underwear
bottoms and a white t-shirt and had apparently just thrown
a chintzy ceramic lamp at Tray's head.

When she turned and saw me, her mouth opened to an
attractive degree and everyone froze.

"Well, at least you didn't go very far." I almost never
have a chance to try out my wise-guy chops. They needed
work.

"Traylor, you idiot. You led him right here." I wasn't
accustomed to hearing such a gravelly voice coming from
such a small woman. This wasn't quite the girl I had

supposedly saved the other night. On closer inspection however, maybe the situation justified the tone.

Her forehead had multiple beads of sweat smearing down towards her eyes, which were more of a subdued grey rather than their natural magnetic blue. When you corner a mouse and hover a boot over his head, you get the same look.

"Alright, first things first; who is this guy?" I motioned towards the cowering Tray with my chin.

"Traylor McCarthy, he's my...boyfriend." I stifled a laugh only because I didn't want to be rude for a change.

Tray relaxed a bit and dropped his arms. He looked a bit like a befuddled gorilla, albeit one who could twist your head off if he got scared.

Just as I was making a mental note that there must be more to this man in some dimension, Stacy decided to take charge of the situation.

"Tray, it's alright, he was hired to protect me. You still shouldn't have brought him here though."

It was a scolding look she gave him, one a mother might give. Maybe he was into that sort of thing. "You can go, I just need to talk with him."

He looked at me like a lost duckling, but hardened up with some effort:

"Alright, but if he starts anything, you know, I'll hear it." He started walking very slowly toward the door. Then he addressed me directly: "I'm not sure where you fit in, but I'm just down below. I saw what was happening and

I did what had to be done. That guy was bad news." He shook his head, tried to peer into my soul through my eyes, failed, and shut the door behind him.

Then it was just a half-naked young Stacy and I. She said:

"So you found me. How?"

"Not in a way anyone would care to replicate, don't worry. Why did you run?"

"I didn't feel safe."

"But Talbot is dead."

"I know, that was Traylor. He didn't like what was happening. He was right."

"There's a first for everything." At least that was one murder solved.

"He may not be too bright, be he at least keeps my interests at heart." Dispassionate would've been one very apt word to describe her tone.

"I don't run into too many women who can take advantage of a man like that, even if it is a man like Traylor. Nice setup Ms. Upton."

She looked at me like I'd tried to brand her with a hot poker. Angry, but tentative.

I continued: "Did you know he was going to kill Talbot?"

"No," she paused and looked like she was going to withdraw, but then I sensed the shield drop, "this is as sober as I've been in a while. When I realized what he'd done, I was still pretty high, so I ran." Her eyes sank and I struggled not to nestle her in my strong arms.

"Alright, well, there's a lot I need to go over with you, but the headline must be that your sister's husband has been killed. Did you...or him, do it?" I nodded toward the office, hoping for a quick answer. No dice.

"No, my God...he's basically been with me since I ran away."

I moved towards her, and she took a half step back.

"They suspect you of killing him, or having him killed." I took a seat on the bed closest to the door, she decided to sit opposite me on the other bed.

"I didn't though," she rubbed her nose with the back of her right hand, stifling a sniffle. "Why would I do that?"

"Well, the police make you as a lead suspect. They intend to find a reason." She looked up at me and put on a helpless kitten look. It's hard to fight weaponry like that, especially when the opponent had the same shimmery azure eyes as I'd gotten used to.

"I'm very tired, Mr. Marsden."

I should've hesitated more, but instead I offered immediately:

"That's alright, I'll go."

As I tensed my legs to stand up she put her hand on my right thigh.

"No, what happens if you tell the police you found me? Stay."

"I won't tell anyone, we're on the same side."

"No, I know you won't if you stay here. Just stay." She did the best impression of her older sister yet. There was little a man could do.

She crawled under the covers of the double bed closest to the bathroom. I started to wonder what good old Traylor McCarthy would think, then she turned off the light. I got under the covers of my own double bed.

■ ■ ■

It was the easiest sleep I'd had in a while.

Light was just about to cross my legs through the same crack in the drapes I'd observed from outside the night before. I looked over at Stacy, who looked like a small kitten wrapped in a scratchy motel blanket. Then my phone binged and I received a text. It was from Quinlin.

"What was that?" The kitten had awoken.

I wanted to answer her, but I wasn't sure myself. It was a very short message that consisted of the words "bad news" and an address. I immediately recognized the place, but didn't want to jump to any conclusions.

I didn't have much trouble convincing Stacy not to accompany me, as she was technically still on the lam. But she did start to get pretty agitated, probably keying off of my own look of intense dread. I said nothing else to her about it and suggested she try to get some more sleep. After leaving her in the less-than-capable hands of Tray, I headed immediately over to the address Quinlin had sent me.

Parking was easy that morning. Everything would get far more complicated from there.

The first time I'd been to the place, I hadn't even noticed a pool around the side of the building, but there it was. A few uniforms, a group of detectives and Quinlin were already on the scene. It struck me how much it looked just like another casual pool party in Los Angeles. Except there was only one person in the pool.

She had a very sleek figure, even under the circumstances. The legs were the giveaway though, like they always had been. The ballerina was floating face down in the pool, naked. It turned out it wasn't a party after all. She was dead.

PART III

The Last Woman

25

"Well, someone should fish her out." Quinlin was never the delicate type.

A plainclothesman with a pool skimmer shimmied up to the edge of the pool and started trying to nudge the ballerina's body toward the mass of law enforcement that had assembled. It was an agonizing process only tempered slightly by the unfortunate presence of several perplexed denizens of the complex.

Some slinked by, some stopped to stare and a plump woman of about forty and definitely unmarried came down to enquire about all the noise. A cop told her and she went stony for about thirty seconds before asking when the pool would be open again.

Finally the body floated its way close enough to the side of the pool to be reeled in by a uniform and an assistant to the medical examiner. The cop with the skimmer gave her one final, gentle poke and the other two men wrestled the body out of the water onto the pool deck.

Bodies occupy a weird place in the human psyche. Throughout history, people have tried to approximate the mass and unwieldy nature of the human body with various items, in an attempt to prepare people for what a completely lifeless individual feels like. They've used potato sacks filled with potatoes, and the same sacks filled with the right amount of sand and filler. Then they tried designing very complicated human replicas out of plastic and silicone. Some even tried hauling around large dead pigs, as they're technically a very close analogue to human flesh. She didn't look like a sack, or a pig for that matter, to me.

I tried to remember what she'd looked like the day we'd made love over and over again in her apartment and just ended up disturbing myself. This thing wasn't a person anymore, and there was nothing I could do about it. I must've looked pretty gloomy, as Quinlin came over and put what I gathered was his version of a comforting hand on my shoulder:

"Well, you got a piece when she was alive at least, right?" He tried to laugh, and then recognized there was a good chance I would drown him in the pool next. "Sorry," he said, and wandered away to find something important to supervise.

An officer and the M.E.'s man had finally turned her over so the initial investigation could begin. There was not a lot of preparation needed, given her distinct lack of clothing. It turned out the only thing that would make an impression on me would be the fact that she didn't have so much as a towel cushioning her head on the concrete pool deck. That and the glaring lack of blue; only the sallow lids, where the blue used to gather.

At first it wasn't immediately evident how she died. The medical examiner pushed his way through the crowd with his kit, got down on one knee and took a long look and a deep breath. He'd seen the scene a million times it seemed, or that's what he wanted to project. He took a long time looking her up and down. I noticed the other men assembled were struggling not to do the same. I decided I didn't need to be coy if everyone else was looking.

All of a sudden the M.E. froze, took out a pair of latex gloves and snapped them on. Then, with just one index finger, he began to prod at the middle of her neck. It was smooth and creamy white. Then his finger pressed down on the skin, and a gush of blood quickly spurted out of a three inch slit in her neck and pooled in between the fine neck muscles that were meant to sustain the skull. You always expect one of the greenhorn cops to get a little queasy around such a sight. I told myself I too was allowed to be queasy in this particular circumstance. The M.E. then motioned for his assistant to cover the body with a sheet, and that was the last I'd ever see of her.

This case had already involved the deaths of two people, but somehow I thought she was simply too pretty to die; this was Hollywood after all. Again I had been wrong though, and now I was in the middle of an explosively expanding case that was too juicy for the media to pass up any longer. More importantly, my client had just turned into a stiff, so I wasn't sure at the moment what I should be doing. I decided the most prudent sort of action would somehow involve a drink as fast as possible.

Before I could move, a wayward honeybee landed on my right hand. It seemed to wander around, probably looking for nectar, but soon flew away without stinging me.

26

I got only the most perfunctory treatment from Quinlin before I left the scene. He looked completely disengaged, and avoided any direct eye contact. On one level I resented his cowardice. On the next level I respected the position he was in and the courtesy he had afforded me by inviting me to the scene. It was his way of showing me he cared. Or that's what I told myself as I stuck the key in the ignition and started my car. I didn't get much further before Quinlin appeared outside my window and knocked. I refocused and lowered it.

He started quietly: "Look Marsden, I know you didn't do it because, well, it was *her*; but they're still gonna think you're a suspect here. It all looks too suspicious."

"I had a feeling."

"You know what the A.D.A would say: stay available."

"I know Quin. You know where to find me."

"I do and I don't. Where were you last night?"

He asked the question but I think he already knew I hadn't been near the ballerina. I'd had enough for that morning, I just couldn't keep up the façade of the hard-boiled guy any more.

"Last night I was with Stacy. I found her." I told him where they could find her. It would at least buy me some time before they decided to question me again. I rolled the window up and primed the engine.

She started moving like she knew where to go, and I was more than slightly relieved to get away from the crime scene. I pushed east back toward my apartment in Hollywood. There was no doubt something I should be doing for my client, or her sister, but I needed a break. It was too bleak.

Before I could decide on a destination my car had deposited herself back in my space under my complex. But there was no way I was going back up to that very quiet, definitely quite lonely apartment.

I took the elevator to street level and struck out into the world. It was a very pleasant day. My watch revealed it was only a little after 12:30 p.m. I made a beeline for the closest, darkest bar I could find.

Unfortunately, I found another bar first. It was an Irish joint that was just a little too new for the 1920s building in which it resided.

The shots were cheap, so I ordered three. They were all brown, so I figured I was on the right track. I topped it off with a well-sourced vodka rocks. It seemed to dissolve the first layer of my esophagus as it went down. I wanted to inform the bartender, but he was preoccupied with one of the actress-waitresses at the other end of the forest green bar top.

The ballerina had bitten the dust, which was tough, but not as tough as the puzzle I had left to assemble. I alone knew the pornographer to be the red-herring of the group of dead folks, thanks to Tray. That left the ballerina's husband and herself as the remaining mysteries. For what it was worth, I didn't blame whoever had killed Mr. Costello. It wasn't fair, but one had to be in the right mood to be fair.

It seemed too convenient for Mrs. Costello to have been murdered by a different person, even if the bodies did end up in very different conditions. Things were starting to smell like a setup, though I had exactly zero proof of such a thing. I decided to run with the conclusion that the same person killed both of them. I didn't know why at the moment, but it felt like a momentous epiphany. I blamed it on the alcohol.

The sun felt much brighter as it beamed in from the boulevard, though I knew it must be at least past the top of its arc by then. I looked around to see who else I could engage in a fruitful conversation.

There were some tourists, probably from the Midwest judging by their accent, sharing a table behind me. They were having a lovely, loud time. Four seats down the bar from me there was a soggy-looking Caucasian man with shriveled dreadlocks. His level of attention was less than stellar, as he struggled to make his pint of beer find his lips. At that moment I felt a bit too crusty for the joint and hopped off my stool.

I was back onto Hollywood Boulevard before I could feel the third shot. I spied the next bar. That's when I fell off a cliff.

27

A foggy recollection:

There's always an answer, right? Always. Books say that, and so does my brain. I hadn't figured out an answer to why my ballerina needed to die. It seemed a bit too sudden to be real.

Of course what was it supposed to be? On my schedule? Damn, those shots went straight up there, didn't they?

I wandered, no, that's not true, I knew where I was going, when I got to the next bar some amount of time later. Staggering would have been generous.

Before I'd settled on my stool, I'd already ordered a bourbon with one rock. Only one. The place was the definition of a hole in the wall. It'd been there forever, and now I was sitting in it. The lighting scheme hadn't been changed since 1962 and that's how they liked it. They being the clientele of course. It was clearly a local's bar. It wasn't exactly pretty, and I'm sure they liked that too, in Hollywood of all places!

The old couple who would drink and die together occupied the end of the bar, both of them faceless. A rocker, who'd seen far more shows than he had ever played, occupied the perch two stools down. Then there was an older gentleman who looked like a hard worker, and drank like one too, judging by the contents his glass. Then there was me. Finally there was the newfangled touchscreen jukebox. Disappointing and lazy.

Wait, I had a phone right in my pocket. Nothing beats looking busy with a fancy phone in LA, except maybe having something to do with it, maybe. I pulled it from my pocket and started flipping around.

Beyond the pointless emails and old voicemails, I got into some trouble. I stumbled into my most recent contact addition; Stacy. I'd taken her number for good reason, because I was responsible. Very. I'd called her earlier with the news of her sister and met a dial tone before I knew what happened. I had to do what I did next, because of the caustic times in which we now live. I resorted to the ambiguity of a text:

"Hey Stacy, hope you're alright." Texts are perfect for imperfect brevity. Really society's fault. Awful. Having said that, punctuation is important. Always.

Silence.

Seconds.

Minutes.

"Hello. I'm sorry, I'm just..kinda out of it. How r you?"

I said something sappy but still manly.

She responded: "Sounds like ur hurting too..."

"I could only imagine."

Or sext.

What a terrible word. It's a combination of two words that converge in a sea of technological garbage.

Before I had a chance to reply with some suitably snappy words, a picture appeared on my screen. It was...fantastic. Of course it must be a dream, because these pictures aren't shooting all over the internet to tireless, desperate drunks and useful boy-toys all the same.

I could tell just what part of the anatomy it was depicting. No, none of those places. Why had a grieving sister sent this to me now? Or why not, at this point...

It was showing just the part of the leg right below a woman's hip. Stacy's hip happens to be perfectly taught. It goes: hip, this little indentation, then the rest of her leg, along with her, well, the spot of course, with a creative twist in the foliage to boot. This groove, not that groove, but this little valley, is perhaps the most beautiful part of the right woman. But the right woman had just died, right? I was starting to spin in circles, and not just because of my stool. I'd just lost the last woman I'd ever really want. Wanted. How do you find another you not just like, not love, not lust after, but want? Wanting is a domain that seems to've been co-opted by spoiled brats and megalomaniacs, sadly. I wanted the ballerina. It was a flaw. A delicious one. I decided to change topics, consciously. I shifted the gear in my sticky head.

Just as I started thinking I'd seen the sign behind the bar in some movie, the bartender came walking back up. I was confused, since I already had a drink, then remembered he probably had no one else to talk to in a place like this at a time like this. I opened my mouth but he snuck in first.

"Everything good?" He was an older man, far older than you'd expect in a Hollywood joint. He was swarthy and unsettlingly trustworthy on the exterior. He wore black slacks, a pressed white shirt and a very classic burgundy vest. I liked the vest, and told him so.

"Thanks boss, I always worn it."

"Oh yeah?"

"Ever since I bought this place. It's a good place. I gotta look good in it, right?"

"Right."

I took a sip of my drink, and he looked up and down the bar, checking on his other patrons. They didn't appear to need his help.

"Been makin' martinis for my father since I was ten."

"No kidding."

"Yup."

"What a classy gent."

"Not at all pal, he was a bastard and a half."

"Oh." All I could think of to do was offer a cheers. He took a moment, looked around, then produced a hidden tumbler of something and took a drink with me.

"You look like you had a tough day man. Let's try something." He took my drained glass away from me. I assumed another round was imminent. It was, but not quite the same. Exciting as it got for me that day. No, wait…the ballerina.

"Negroni. I know how to make em', just like the old days, heh." He chuckled to himself as he mixed the drink.

The thing about Negronis is that they're hard to drink. I've never met one I liked, but I never met one I didn't drink, either. Today was not a day to stop drinking.

He clinked the glass with the shaker and pushed it over the copper-topped bar in my direction. I swayed and caught it. I moved to produce a wallet but…

"No, no sir. I mixed it just for you, I'd like you to enjoy it, all the way."

"You sure?"

"You need it most out of all out of these people."

I looked around again to make sure I was indeed in the most need. I could see no one who could need it more, though none that would've rejected it. I drank and my taste buds packed up. Luckily, it was about that time of day.

"Great."

He seemed satisfied. "I know, eh? A great drink for a day like today."

"What's a day like today?"

"Not smooth man, not smooth."

The drink wasn't smooth either. I took a whiff and was immediately reminded of chlorine. Then I remembered the pool, then I remembered her. I guess I still wasn't feeling it, so I moved on.

It was starting to get dark. Dark. That I could relate to.

I looked west down the boulevard. It was a choice picture alright. The sun was hitting the hills just right, and through the palms it reflected back into my eyes. It hurt a little given my liquor intake. So what?

The next place. I decided to try my luck. Luck was supposed to hit at some point, I hadn't had any in forever.

It was a little brighter than I would've liked, but it was a slightly classier place too. Hey, I was wearing pants, no problem there. Pink drapes framed the windows that looked out onto Cahuenga. There was some sort of postmodern dance number on a television suspended from a corner of the ceiling. A smarmy bartender struggled to mix a highball as two less than interested customers watched passively. Somebody had let two chauffeurs in; but seriously, who wears a suit in Hollywood? Then I saw her.

Wait.

I say that like it was a blow to the head. A blow. Not… that.

There's always a new storyline; always.

I perched myself on a stool next to her. She was a few years younger than me, and sat like she'd learned to cross her legs only days before. She had a pretty face, some brunette hair (a little stringy) and I'll admit she had some tits to boot. Odd.

The rest of her was good enough. A solid B straight away. Prime.

She was just alluring enough to be upsetting, but I didn't know that yet.

"Hey there, what ya drinking?" I didn't need to be all hardboiled all the time, no one's gotta know. A drink appeared in front of me from an annoying shape who finally went away after I shoved some plastic at him.

"Oh, just a fruity thing. A girl's drink." She was so happy to talk, so happy.

"No need to disparage yourself." My stupid grin grew a little too fast. But it didn't matter.

"Oh you're funny." A smile trying to be coy enough to be interesting.

"Where are you from?"

"Ohio."

"Oh yeah? Where in Ohio?"

"You wouldn't know it, it's alright, just...Ohio"

"Try me. Cleveland's not that small." I patted my brain on the back.

"Ha. Close to there actually. So what do you do?" That was fast.

"I'm a private detective."

"Oooohhh!" It was like a hummingbird landing on my eardrums. "Just like out of the movies. Bogart and stuff!"

"Yup, pretty much."

All of a sudden my patience ran out. It's like someone had bored a hole straight through me and my ability to sop up mediocrity had leaked out. I started to figure what her thighs might look like from a different angle.

"So where are you staying?"

"Oh just a small place, a few blocks over."

"I'd like to see it, I love small places."

Her eyes said sure, and the rest of her was about to say the same, then Ohio came screaming back.

"Oh um, wow, well...can I get your number?" A girl asking for my number; could be worse. Could be much better if she just skipped it.

I gave her my number and she excused herself to the restroom.

"Damn, that didn't take long at all." Another brunette, this time a familiar one. My favorite liquor slinger Tina had seen the whole shebang. "She's not coming back."

"Or she's just getting ready for me."

Her cheeks pulled hard on the corners of her mouth, slowly at first, speeding up. Another hint of hope?

Tina I'd known for a while. Not long, but just long enough. She bought me a drink. I bought her a drink. She rotated through the other customers. I shifted after my third drink and looked at the clock. It had mysteriously ticked off several hours in about twenty minutes.

"So, what's new with you Duncan?" Innocent? I almost spit out my drink.

"Ha. Quite a last few days. You know my glamorous life."

"Toilet stop up again?" She was trying too hard. She always tried too hard. It hurt my head, but I couldn't resist it at this point. Couldn't.

"One of my clients just packed up and left."

"Left? Like, LA?"

"Like, this mortal coil."

"Where?" She was a bartender. But she was still pretty cute. Long, very light brown hair, a high, dignified fore-head and actually some not awful bluish eyes. –Ish... Her jeans fit pretty well, so that was alright. Her t-shirt was tight and her thigh-high boots weren't bad either. She saw what I was looking at and didn't move to hide it.

"She died."

"Oh damn."

"Yup. But that just means case is over, no more money for Mr. Marsden this week."

"Well, next one's on me then, again..." She always had an edge, it's why I'd known her all these months, presumably.

We each did a shot and the clock hovered nervously in the moments around midnight. The big one-two...

I met her outside and she lit a cigarette. Nothing fancy, just a solid smoke.

"I'll walk you back, it is Hollywood after all."

"Oh that's okay; I normally don't walk back anyway."

"Which way is it?" I presented my arm and she put hers through it. We started to walk.

"I guess you never know who could be around the next corner. Some guy did get shot around here a few weeks ago."

"There are a million ways to die around the corner, what's so bad about a bullet?" I immediately thought I'd been a bit too dark, but I'd be lying if I didn't fantasize a little about a nosy gun barrel finding its way to my temple.

But hey, at least there was a girl on my arm. That's what the unfathomably positive would say.

We didn't talk anymore. It was just another warm night in Hollywood with a girl I liked. Liked is what I needed to say.

■ ■ ■

It was messy. It was hot. The air-conditioning didn't work. It never worked. The light was off but the light from the street was just enough to tell what was going on. I was inside her. I will say she was always wet, very wet; always self-conscious about it.

She looked up at me, and appeared to be enjoying what was happening. Her eyes would flick open, then close again. She'd moan and look up at me. I watched through my eyes, then through hers. This was sex, the kind everyone settles for. It definitely wasn't bad, but, well, it wasn't bad, I guess.

After a substantial amount of time, I rolled onto my back, and she hopped on top. There really was a little hop. Then she went sensual. She controlled her level of penetration very carefully. A little more this time, a little less that time, always speeding up. I was thinking an awful lot. It was really warm in her bedroom...

Finally I had an ounce of strength and flipped her off me and onto her stomach. She re-positioned herself and waited. To my own surprise, that was all I needed. I re-entered her and she moaned again. Then again and again.

I sped up and so did she. It was going pretty well. Then she stopped moaning. I got a little worried. Then I used my investigative skills, and realized she had passed out. I stopped and sat there. The light from a traffic light outside changed from a dazzling green, to a somber red. The orange street light stayed the same color it had always been. I sat there naked, breathing. Quietly.

28

Water was good. Really good. Even for LA water. Maybe it was the pipes. I started to get myself back together.

Tina still lay naked and passed out in her bedroom, but that was nothing new. I wished it had gotten old at some point, but I hadn't had much choice the way I saw it. A man can't turn down even a moderately attractive girl, especially not in the state I was in. Some men never get the chance to have the kind of sex I had. I was not going to give it up for a dead woman, not now.

Another glass of water. The boiling blood and my broiled brain were cooling off some more. I was surprised I didn't have a headache. Then I reminded myself not to get too cocky, I still had a long way to go no doubt.

I slowly dressed, hoping she'd wake up so I could seal things up like usual. Nothing too outlandish, I just liked to have my ducks in a row. Another glass…

Ten minutes later and I was feeling like a new enough man that I could venture back out into the world. Tina slept on, and I made a stealthy escape out onto the landing and then down the stairs and onto the street. I started walking back toward the center of Hollywood. It was still only 1 a.m. Still time for something to happen.

I came upon a homeless man lounging on an abandoned textile couch. It was collapsed, but he didn't seem to mind. He was laughing. Not just laughing, but wholeheartedly buying into the idea that life was funny. I didn't think I'd ever be able to feel the ecstasy he was feeling. I moved on.

Next up, I crossed a freeway off ramp. There weren't any cars, but there was still a warm whoosh of air coming off baked asphalt. It was actually quite calming, bordering on refreshing.

It reminded me of the Santa Ana winds. Those infamous gusts that either brought redemption in the form of unexpected change, or just the downright snuffing of civil values, depending on whom you ask. At least it's movement.

I wasn't really headed anywhere; I'd done all the bars I thought I could handle that night. Sure it'd got me laid, but that was literally it. A black cloud was still pressing me into the pavement. Then I had a novel thought.

I dashed across the street and made my way up to the second story of a battered strip mall. The pool hall entrance was illuminated only by a neon sign advertising lite beer. This was a simple spot; I already felt better.

I walked in and took a look around. My cockles were warmed by the scene:

A woman who could've bitten through a beer bottle sat behind a front desk facing away from the door. She watched a Spanish language version of a popular TV sit-com. The voices were all off and she looked like she didn't mind. The rest of the place was mostly deserted, save for one billiard table with four men standing around it contemplating a shot. Two of the men looked "biker," two looked pretty straight-laced. Inexplicably, some choice soul music was playing out of a speaker somewhere. I stepped up to the counter.

"How much to play?" The operator turned around and gave me the once-over. She tapped a sign above her head with a broken pool cue: 1 game, $10 with a drink, $7 without. I opted for the former and gave her my request for vodka.

"Only beer." Without slowing down in the slightest, she popped the cap off a bottle and slid a tray of balls over the counter. I paid without protest.

I made my way over to an empty table, removed the cover and turned on the overhead chandelier light. The green felt consumed my vision. Just a flat, predictable rectangle. A comforting sight for a depressed detective.

Chalk? Check. Cue? Dented but workable. I tipped the tray and spread the spheres around with my hands. The men at the other table looked up with the smallest glimmer of interest, then went back to their own activities.

I racked and took some big steps toward the end of the table to break. I swiveled and:

"Hey buddy, I'll play ya."

I turned and saw a man who'd shaved maybe three days before, with a slack jaw and some downright mean-looking eyes. He was about six-three, and thick in the places that would make him a formidable opponent for all but a machete wielding titan. He had an unlit cigarette wedged between two thin sheets of lip. The rest of him looked fittingly rough.

"Wasn't looking for a game in fact." I took a swig of beer, remembered it was lite, and put it on the table behind me.

"Hey, you don't have to be lookin' for a game. I'm just sayin'."

"Alright, sure pal. Got a cue?" He produced one from behind his broad back. I nodded in agreement that he did, in fact, somehow have a cue back there. He then leaned over, gobbled all the balls into the crook of his arm and ushered them into a corner. I set up to lag for the break.

He joined me at the end of the table and stood waiting, staring. It was slightly odd, but then I still had more alcohol than blood in my veins.

I pulled back and-

"I take it you got an interesting case on your hands."

The abrupt nature of his comment was meant to botch both my shot and my composure. Bingo.

I shanked the lag and my jaw must've hit my toes, as he chuckled a bit and stopped the cue ball half way across

the table, drawing it back toward him. Not great Marsden, not cool at all.

"Eh, keep it together-it's Marsden, right?" He smiled but kept the cigarette clamped.

"Yeah." I wasn't giving him anything.

"Hey, relax. I'm a dick from Connecticut." Connecticut; he was laying it out for me, very charitable.

"Always good to hear the lingo. What brings you to LA?"

"I think you know why huh? I got hired by a broad to look for her husband, Daniel Upton."

"You don't say." I didn't want to give him the satisfaction, but I had a feeling he'd already gotten his fill and then some if he'd been watching me for any length of time.

"I do. She told me who you were, I figured we could put in together, you know, up our margins and shit." He finally removed the cigarette from his mouth for effect.

"Were you following me all night?"

"Since ya left the crime scene this morning. Naked, dead girl floating in a pool? That kinda news is hard to hide in this town I guess. You lead an interestin' life."

"Thank God."

"So where we at? Can we throw in together?"

"Maybe pal, maybe. I just have to hit the can, I'll be right back, then let's talk." The way he studied my face he must've thought I was going to blow chunks right there since he let me leave without any more questions.

I slammed into the dank, cramped "restroom" as the sign on the door so optimistically proclaimed and found the lone stall. Almost hit my knees, then looked at the state of the dirty tile floor and decided a squat was more in order as I upchucked what felt like the last few nights' worth of meals and liquor into the toilet.

After about three more acid baths, my esophagus was beat and I'd sweat through my shirt. I had a bit more time to survey my surroundings. They were as unimpressive as I'd initially assumed. Cracked mirror, some wantonly creative graffiti on the tile walls. It was classic; the bathroom with the creaky fan that will struggle for eternity and never manage to get that smell out...never.

I stood up, felt slightly better, and whipped my brain into action. This guy, who I realized hadn't even revealed his name, apparently knew me, the Upton situation, or at least some of it, and had the ability to find me in the middle of Hollywood at 1:27 a.m. in the morning. It didn't seem good at all. Then again, with all that had happened, I didn't even know what I was supposed to be doing anyway. Sometimes you have to be willing to fall off the edge, or at least hold on for dear life as the wind whips you around a little.

I strolled back out, adjusting my collar as if I'd powdered my nose, and got back into the game. I opted to let the guy break, and break he did. Two solids and a stripe. Never a good sign, but nothing I couldn't bounce back from.

"So, who are you?" I started subtle.

"Jackson Comor, I guess I shoulda started with that, ha." He was already enjoying himself as he sank another solid in the corner pocket. Then he lined up for his next shot. A doozy; two stripes into a solid into the pocket. It struck me how much the balls reminded me of the players in my terrible case. Then I was struck by what a stilted thought that was.

He sank another, but the thoughts remained. Stacy, the pornographer, Mr. Costello and the ballerina were all involved. Everyone had an inkling that they were all connected, they just didn't have the right combination. Neither did I for that matter, but seeing them all lined up like that on the felt made me sure it was true. There was a through line I was missing. Lite beer was no good for sussing things like that.

"So buddy, how's the case really going? I was just brung in to find the husband, but I hear you're out to find the younger daughter huh?" He finally took a shot and missed, banking off the far rail.

"Yeah, well, it's all a mess now. Whole case is really shot to hell."

"Why's that?"

I was supposed to be good at obscuring, but instead I just got agitated. Something didn't sit right. He did have some knowledge of the situation, but I was trying to trust my queasy gut. It still mattered in my assessment of things every now and again.

"Eh, just that the *broad* you said hired you, Mrs. Upton, came by my office and tried to say she wasn't looking for her husband. So it's a little odd you showing up is all." It was unrelated to his question, but I was trying to redirect, clumsily.

"What does that have to do with your case buddy? I know that stiff in the pool this morning was Mrs. Upton's oldest kid. Don't try to snow me." He paused his motion. I decided to take a shot and up the drama. I took aim at a stripe in another corner…and missed, badly.

"Look, it's just that you showing up here-" I didn't get a chance to finish, as my phone stepped in to break up the conversation. I looked down and saw a familiar downtown number. I answered: "Hello?"

"Well, glad to see you're still awake and on the case. We got the girl, Stacy, just where you told us she was. We had to pummel her boyfriend a little." I cracked a smile, not that Quinlin could see.

"Find anything out?"

"Nothing from the girl, she's just young and afraid and all that kind of thing. Useless. However, we did toss her place and found some cash in envelopes."

"Envelopes eh? Jackpot." I was pleased with myself that I could still muster some sarcasm after the day I'd had.

"Quiet down. Talbot's cheesy porn logo is stamped on all of them. But looks like they've been recycled. There's an interesting address on at least three of them; someone tried to cross it out with a marker, but it's there. We found some other strange correspondence with the same address at Talbot's house. Cryptic stuff. Thought we could swing by to check out the place, after you come pick her up, of course." There was a grin in his voice, as though he knew I'd be there for Stacy in a heartbeat. I agreed and hung up. I guess I was smiling.

"Squeegee that grin off your face buddy. It's your turn and your turn to cough up some info. Who was that?"

"How bout' I do you one better. I have to go do a chore, but why don't we meet at the Mad Miracles lounge tomorrow afternoon and we talk some shop. I'm not opposed to it."

He looked through slits at me for a long enough time to make me uncomfortable. Finally he agreed, we exchanged information and I quickly gathered my stuff and ducked out into the night. It was pretty foggy. I tried to like it, like people in San Francisco claim to, and failed.

29

I somehow managed to weakly jog all the way back to my complex and headed immediately to my car. I figured I was just marginal enough to drive after emptying the contents of my stomach three times.

I roared out with a renewed sense of purpose, mostly because someone had actually given me one.

On the way down the 101 towards headquarters, I glimpsed a rather foreboding object out of the passenger side window to the west. The moon was yellowed, brittle. It looked like it had burnt out and was slowly tumbling into the sea. My vigor muted slightly, I continued on with a more demure mindset.

It was so demure that I neglected to even dissect my odd meeting with the peculiarly intimidating Mr. Comor. I was willing to bet he was only from Connecticut by way of New Jersey, judging by his rather telling wise-guy accent. It didn't mean he wasn't a PI. It did mean I finally had found at least one concrete reason to not trust him. That made me feel a little better, then my stomach promptly found a way to make me feel a little worse. I cringed and gingerly stabbed at the throttle to get the trip over with.

I parked at a meter and unsteadily made my way across to the very familiar city hall. I walked in and noticed one very bored security guard sitting in a small vestibule, on his phone, or maybe just pretending. Either way, I ignored him and, just as I'd done days before, rode once again to the fifth floor. This time the doors opened to an eerily empty reception area. The bulbous-eyed receptionist wasn't there, probably because it was a little after 2 a.m. I consciously made some small improvements to my very rumpled outfit and pressed down the hall toward the assistant D.A.'s office. Before I had a chance to make a grand entrance, the door popped outward and Quinlin immediately put a finger to his lips as he closed the door behind him. I waited for the update.

"We've had her for about five hours now, and she's given us exactly nothing. You know what her deal is?"

I didn't have the energy for obfuscation: "I don't think she has a deal. Her sister is dead and presumably her boyfriend is in custody for at least one murder?"

Quinlin's fat head bobbed up and down a measured amount.

"You're just letting a possible accessory-or worse-go? What kind of flip flopper is this assistant D.A.? Stacy won't get to experience the wonderful hospitality like I did."

"You're a little less fragile than her. Having said that, yes he's cutting her loose. Right now she's clammed up pretty good, and obviously pretty damn upset. Nothing more she's going to show or tell us in here. He wants to see if she can generate some leads for us."

"How reasonable of you all." I would've sneered, if my face muscles had possessed the stamina at that point in the evening. "That's almost some fine police work."

Quinlin just grinned and his chins quivered.

"So? What're we waiting for?" I moved toward the door again. Quinlin put out his hand, put an ear to the door. Satisfied, he opened it for me. I strolled into fabulous company.

Rodriguez sat exactly where he did for my interview, and looked like more chair than man at this point. His fingers were still tapping a pen. I guessed he hadn't been allowed to illicitly smoke in quite some time. Of course my favorite duo, Donnelly and Pudgy, were there too, but looked pretty tired and probably more than ready to throw their quarry to me and catch some z's. Donnelly didn't even look up when I walked in, nor did he treat me to some folksy repartee. He just packed up and walked by me nonchalantly. Pudgy followed him out, grinning of course. Then it was just Rodriguez, Quinlin, a stenographer and a small framed woman, who appeared physically broken from within: Stacy Upton.

She only turned her head, and just a tinge of her blue irises escaped from her very red and puffy eyelids. From the look of her makeup, she had cried about forty gallons of tears directly onto the assistant D.A.'s floor.

Then I was overtaken by a new feeling of grief and dazzling rage.

"Another successful interrogation." I cursed with more vitriol than I'd even intended.

Quinlin started, "Duncan, for God's sake-"

The assistant D.A. interrupted instead, "yeah thanks Mr. Marsden. Just get her out of here." I felt like I should come up with a rancorous comeback, but then I glanced at Stacy, who looked like she was about to bleed more tears, and the wind left my sails. I reached my hand out and she gingerly took it and stood up on wobbly legs. They had given her a pair of police issue sweats and her shirt looked like the one I had left her wearing the day before. She clung to her purse like it held the Holy Grail. Even the smallest movement seemed to take all the effort she could muster.

I tried to be as protective as I could while giving the D.A. what I judged to be a superior stink eye. We walked out, my arm around her narrow shoulders. Some tears still misted her lashes as we crossed the threshold into the hall. For effect, I slammed the door behind me, as more profanity flooded my consciousness.

However, before I could even enjoy my awesome act of rebellion, Quinlin popped the door back open and closed it behind him.

"Marsden, one more word." He stood there, expectantly waiting for me to come to him. I nodded toward the now apparently catatonic Stacy. I delicately leaned

her against the wall and walked back over to Quinlin. He
sounded a little desperate:

"Alright, so you've got her now. I know what you must
be thinking, given what you just saw-"

"Long night."

"Long day, damn it." He took out his handkerchief,
then refolded it and replaced it inside his sport coat. He
looked relieved, then got serious again as he looked me in
the eye. "You should start carrying your piece. I know everyone thinks they got a bead on things, but I know this
is bound to spiral out of control, and you have the cata-
lyst right there." He looked up toward Stacy, then quickly
averted his gaze.

"Great."

"I'm serious. Duncan, there's a force here that we can't
account for; I'm willing to back you if anything happens.
Just go home and get it before you do anything else. This
is going to bust wide open, and I'd like to avoid your head
being the thing busted, if we can."

"Very nice of you." I was still seething from before, so
I didn't have a lot of faith left in the justice system at that
moment.

"Duncan, have I screwed you over, ever, really?
Really?" He really seemed to want an answer too.

"I'll go home first, take her home, then catch some
shut eye. I'll call you to go after that address from the envelopes tomorrow."

He breathed what I decided to interpret as a sigh of
relief. Then he smiled, clapped me on the back and sent

me toward the dark little shape that was Stacy. He slipped back into the office. It was quiet, punctuated by sniffles. And one sigh.

30

The walk to the car was silent and felt like tiptoeing over broken glass. I wasn't sure about anything; what Stacy knew, what she had told them, what she expected now, whether I could manage to not throw up again before Hollywood. Time to chance it.

I remotely unlocked the doors and suavely pulled the passenger side open for her. She didn't even bother to look me in the eye as she slumped into the car. Without hesitating she simply bent her knees and melted into the passenger seat without so much as a breath. I took that as a small victory toward my goal of getting my shit back together, and bounced around to the driver side. I entered. Still nothing from the girl. Good.

I turned the key, and growled down toward the 101 north onramp. She was glued straight ahead-maybe this would be more painless than I thought, or deserved.

"You son of a bitch, you sold me out." She was still looking forward, her voice was calloused. So much for painless.

"Not really." The retort was shabby for a thirteen year old, so for me it was downright pitiful. I deserved what came next.

But there was nothing. Nothing. She looked like she was going to rocket through the sunroof, but she still didn't say anything.

I offered: "I didn't give you up. Well, I did, but it wasn't a big deal. Your idiot boyfriend was going to catch it at some point anyway. I didn't have a choice, you're safer now." I felt more pathetic by the second.

We whizzed by the Santa Monica Boulevard exit and I looked at her out of the corner of my eye. She still sat there, like a subtle statue. I was waiting for the explosion of emotion that I knew was brewing behind her now gunmetal eyes, but I had a feeling I wasn't going to get the payout that night.

Inexplicably, she cracked a very slight grin. Her pallor changed to a healthier-type glow, and I tried to identify the source of her apparent optimism. But it seemed to be emanating directly from within her. That was unsettling.

Finally we reached Hollywood, and I guided us through the now silent streets. The last bits of the faded moon from before were just receding behind the Santa Monica Mountains as we entered my parking garage.

"Why are we here? I thought you were taking me home."

"This is just going to be a quick stop. I was told that we should protect ourselves from here on out. I thought, why start bending the rules now." I could tell she wanted to quiz me on my vague and rather useless response, but for some reason she again held her tongue. Once we parked, she carefully opened her door and wafted out in the direction of the elevators. I removed the key from the ignition, took a deep breath and followed her.

■ ■ ■

The elevator ride was about as interesting as the car trip from downtown. She stared straight ahead, and as the doors dinged open, followed me down the hall to my apartment. I looked back at her several times, but it was quite clear she was not focusing on me, not even a bit.

Clicking the lock open, I beckoned her to follow me inside, which she did. She immediately drifted over to the couch and sat down. I offered her a drink, but she just shook her head.

"Alright, well, I'll be right back; I just need to get our protection." I wasn't sure why I said it so provocatively, but it didn't matter, as it failed to illicit any real response from her. Stacy was made of stone, and there was nothing I could do about it. Then I thought about the alluring picture she'd sent me when I was at the bar. I did want to ask her why she'd sent it, but I counseled myself that it would probably be best to delay that question for the time being.

I went to my bed, felt around under the dust ruffle and found what I was looking for. I dragged out the metal lockbox and produced my janitor-spec keychain. After fumbling through about twenty years' worth of keys, I found the one I was looking for, and carefully inserted it into the lock.

Inside was my perfectly preserved Colt M1911 .45 caliber pistol. I'd fired it every few months for the past few years ever since I'd found it sitting stiffly in one of the family's forgotten boxes, but I still had yet to use her against anyone I cared to be rid of. Most people will say a .45 is overkill in this day and age. I never understood the term.

I pulled it out, found a neighboring box containing ammunition, clicked in the clip and wrestled on my underarm holster. In theory, I was safer; I'd done exactly what Quin had told me to do. My head started to hurt again. I remembered where I'd been earlier that night and immediately felt more fatigued. I slowly made my way back out to the living room to deal with Stacy.

There wasn't much to deal with as it turned out. Stacy had curled herself up on the sofa and gone to sleep. I thought she might just have been lying down, but as I approached her I realized she was completely out. Her face was to the cushions. I could see her ribcage slowly rise and fall. Such a fragile creature. I carefully tiptoed to the kitchen and mixed myself a stiff highball. I looked out the window and saw my familiar palm tree. A beautiful sheen of Hollywood night light reflected on the fronds. I took a big gulp and headed back into the living room to take a load off.

I removed my coat, but left my holster on. It made me feel pretty good, especially with the drink in one hand. It's one of the most powerful positions for a man to be in, I decided. Watching over a sleeping girl with a gun and a drink: my job.

Then I started swirling away. I could see her tight ass through the thin police issue sweats. I noticed how the curve of her back embraced her tight t-shirt.

There she was, one of those one-in-a-million girls, sleeping right on my couch. At least that was something. I might not be getting paid, but it was something...

Before I could take my thoughts further into the abyss, I'd finished my highball and decided to rest my eyes, just for a moment. Such a warm, perfect darkness.

31

My eye rest came to an abrupt end with a shake and some surly sighs. I cracked my lids and saw that it was just starting to get light out.

Stacy was standing over me and looked like she'd been up for a while. "Okay Marsden, let's go. I'm tired and your couch is like sleeping on a pile of gravel. I want my bed."

I didn't even have a chance to fight her, not that I had the energy. I felt along my pants leg and found my car keys. I stretched, to show I was making progress, and she turned to gather up her things.

We made our way slowly back down to my car as I carefully massaged the sleep out of my eyes.

I pulled us out onto the boulevard and headed west. Back on her street, I miraculously found a spot vacated by some sucker who probably had to get to work at 5 a.m. I positioned myself to park.

"You don't have to come in; I think we're all in agreement as to where I live and where I can be found." I ignored her and paralleled before she could extricate herself. She cracked that same mysterious semi-grin from the previous night and saved the rest of whatever she meant to say.

"Hey, I gotta show I'm still useful, right?" It felt like I was dropping her off after a bad date. I guess it kind of was, in my mind. I did pause a moment as I watched her get out, which turned out to be a rewarding show. She pursed her lips as she pulled herself from the vehicle, showing off her brilliant backside in the process. I was running a bit low on shame apparently.

Up to the front entrance of her building, then up the stairs to her apartment. I felt like an unwanted appendage, but I just couldn't give her up yet. Maybe I'd lost one too many beautiful women in the last twenty four hours.

She rooted around in her designer purse and came up with her set of keys, which she then slid into the lock. I took a long blink. At least something was done, for now.

Bang. I thought she'd just opened the door a little too fast, but then I itched next to my eye and came back with blood on my fingers. Stacy looked up at me and could only offer some wide eyes and an impression of a stiff. I pushed her out of the doorway and she fell back onto the landing with a "yelp." So she was still alive; this could still turn out alright for Marsden. I'd had a pretty bad record recently.

I dove down into the apartment and could feel electricity run up and down the length of my frame as I reached for the Colt under my arm. I saw a shape withdraw behind a table that had been toppled onto its side. I snickered to myself, un-holstered my piece and shot directly at the table. Observers would no doubt laugh to themselves, until they realized I was firing a real .45, which could punch clear through the chintzy piece of furniture. The gunshots snapped me into comprehending what was actually happening, and the last dregs of alcohol instantly evaporated from my system.

There was a bit of grunting from behind the table and then I saw a black pistol shape emerge and haphazardly aim in my direction. I fired again and strategically rolled to my left, into what turned out to be the kitchen.

It was dirty. I saw a roach carcass under a decrepit cabinet. Before anyone else could shoot at me, I was able to right myself back onto my feet. I heard some wet coughing and patted myself on the back for some apparently fantastic shooting. Then I noticed the kitchen was of the pass-through variety. I elevated my gun and slowly made my way through the back entrance. Inching out, I slowly swung right to try to flank whoever it was that was doing all the shooting.

I turned the corner to find a man crumpled into a ball, a pool of blood emanating from his midsection. The shape did look oddly familiar. Some billiard balls knocked their way through my mind, but I couldn't concentrate.

What a turn of events. I had shot a man I couldn't even see through a solid wood table. Not too shabby.

Another bang. Too soon to celebrate. I was new at the whole shoot-out thing after all. At least at the returning fire part. Damn it.

A shot probably meant for my head crashed through the drywall just to my right and covered me in dust. I tried to take a breath and re-aim, but I coughed and fell down instead. I fired anyway, in the general direction of the threat, but to no avail. When I looked up from my knees, whoever he was had disappeared, leaving behind a pool of blood, several shell casings and a smell of burned flesh. I took a moment to compose myself, then struggled to my feet and sprinted back to the door. No perp. But Stacy? I couldn't look.

"Jesus Christ!" She was more annoyed than anything, which made me smile. Having confirmed Stacy was very much alive, I immediately headed for the rear balcony, which I identified as the shooter's escape route. Where had the bastard gone? I knew him; I just needed to place him.

"Who was that? Why are they trying to kill *me* now!?" Some more hysterical questions later, and I turned back to a shaken, but oddly rejuvenated Stacy. She was combing some wood splinters out of her hair with her lanky fingers. Somehow it struck me as sexy in spite of the circumstances.

I dragged her over the threshold and bolted the door. She took a seat on her shabby couch and looked over the destruction.

"Sorry for the-"

"Save it Marsden. I know what you're going to say, and you're not smooth enough." Ouch. I decided to chalk it up to her partially destroyed apartment. I clicked the safety back on my gun and re-holstered it under my left arm. Of course the lull caused her to burst into tears. Adrenaline was still pumping though, nothing I couldn't handle. I went over and sat myself right next to her and attempted to shelter her against my body. She didn't like that one bit.

"Damn it! Stop it!" She pushed me away and covered her face with her hands. Then I knew I'd touched a nerve, one that I'd probably been aware of the whole time.

It looked fake, but I knew it was real; she was crying, and not just because of the bullet shower moments earlier. "It's alright-," I didn't have many arrows in my quiver at that point.

She furiously dug through her purse and jabbed a ragged five by seven photograph at me. Black and white. The scenery looked familiar, like from the original naked photos of the young ballerina I'd found in the file at the pornographer's house. This picture looked like it had been folded and re-folded about a thousand times. I almost lost it, since I hadn't seen her since her murder. Then there was the rest.

The naked ballerina, minus about ten years, was bound to a chair, with what looked like leather belts. She was looking directly at the camera. Her ass was up in the air, and her sister stood behind her, confused but still holding a broken broomstick.

It was a grotesque fantasy. THE fantasy. It was excruciating. My ballerina and her sister, the ideal, naked, in front of me. Forbidden. Young. Damn it. I thought about asking for a drink. Instead I teared up. I didn't even try to stop it. By the time I knew what I was doing, she'd already seen me. I partially crumpled up the picture and dropped it on the ground. I wasn't going to give up my moral standing that easily. I had a gun after all. I could still see the ballerina's nude leg on the floor.

"It was our father, alright! It was him. He was our first ballet teacher."

"I didn't even know you-"

"Oh yes you did you asshole. Both me and my sister danced. He was our first dance teacher, he did everything for us. Both of us. Just, he did stuff to us too. Damaged both of us. Just...well look at it. God damn it!" She couldn't put anything else into words, and just tried to hit me a few times. She hit my arm pretty hard, and normally I would've legitimately complained, but a strange numbness had descended over my whole body.

I put my arm around her, treating her like a rare artifact. I'd watched on TV somewhere you weren't supposed to do that with a victim, and should instead always treat them like a real person. But she wasn't. She wasn't real just then, and I didn't want her to be. Then I realized I was floating a little too far out of reality. I gripped her shoulder a little harder. She tried to recoil and I didn't let her.

Then she spilled everything: "The cops don't get it at all. My father killed my sister, killed her husband, he's the guy everyone's after. I know it. He sent me that picture last month. I thought he'd gotten past it. Moved on. Maybe to someone else."

Her naiveté would've been adorable had it not been for the rotten subject matter. She told me everything she'd told the LAPD:

"I told them everything; I cracked like it was nothing." She wiped some tears away, and continued. "I told them how my father used me and my sister since I was seven and she was twelve. We never had a chance, but then again, because of our family's resources, we had every chance. Boy does that sound lame. They didn't really get it, I think."

Maybe I didn't want to believe that the ballerina's past contained this visceral level of cruelty. I went back and forth on the ramifications and decided none of them mattered. Jesus, I'd never been in love with anyone, let alone a dead woman, and now this.

Stacy continued to detail all the abuse that she had endured. I believed every detail of it. It all made too much sense. I tried to check myself and remain professionally skeptical. Then I realized that even if a fraction of it were true, it would be too much. I picked up the crumpled photo off the floor. Its glossy finish shined. I walked over to the decrepit, unused fireplace, found some matches, and lit it on fire. I threw it into the fireplace and walked back over to Stacy as it quickly turned into a mess of curled ashes. She looked up with hollow, grey eyes and waited for my assessment. I bent down, wanted to kiss her, and pecked her on the cheek instead. Then I stomped out of her apartment. I heard sirens in the distance, getting closer. My brain was pretty damn drained... and boiling.

32

I got to my car, opened the door, and sank into the seat. There weren't a lot of moves left. The abuse leveled against the ballerina and her sister was horrific; it was all pretty life shattering. But something still bothered me, and at that early hour, it was extremely difficult to deduce what it was. Something about the man in the coffee shop I'd seen, the girls' father, didn't scream unfettered murderer. He might've been a narcissistic, incestuous sociopath, , but he didn't seem capable of liquidating his own family, especially considering his unhealthy, and apparently unquenchable, desire for them. Then I got a hunch as to the source of the bad vibes. I rifled through my pockets and found the key card with "The Roosevelt" printed on it that Mrs. Upton had dropped in my office. Before I could second guess my-self, I tossed on a pair of sunglasses and peeled out.

Traffic was just starting to pick up as I snaked my way through Hollywood toward my destination.

There's no other way to put it, the Roosevelt Hotel is an imposing building. It's the first thing that pops up when you type "the Roosevelt" into a search engine, which is unfortunately a measure of some substance these days. You'd think the first thing would at least be something about a president, but no, it's the hotel.

It's gorgeous though. The neon sign on the roof still serves as a Polaris for the desperate souls of Tinseltown. It's authentic and significant without being a touristy morass, mostly because interesting people continue to use it as a destination, as opposed to just stay there out of necessity.

The Spanish Colonial colossus still stands, after salacious scandal and unsympathetic earthquake alike. Its pale sand-colored walls house so much unadulterated Hollywood history it threatens to spill out the old front doors onto the boulevard daily. All that, and I was no stranger to drinking there either.

I pulled up, and a slim valet with a shiny crimson vest and greasy black spiked hair opened my door.

"Welcome to the Roosevelt." He seemed to beckon me in with all the fanfare of a depressed ringmaster.

"Thanks, put it on Upton." I stepped out and took an invigorating breath.

"I'm sorry sir, but what room would that be?"

All of a sudden I felt completely on point: "What? Jesus, I don't know, hey, HEY!" I got the attention of the head bellman, who looked stunned to have been addressed at all. "What room is Upton? That's my room."

His bald head started to sweat, as the spikey haired valet just stood there, awaiting instructions from anyone. Of course the bellman should never reveal a room number to some schmuck, but I felt good that morning.

"You're Mrs. Claire Upton?" He decided to make a thing out of it. I was a little surprised, but decided to stick to my guns. I removed my sunglasses and gave a stare to melt steel.

"You in the business of being in my business?" That sounded pretty hardboiled.

He crumbled satisfyingly and quickly glanced at a computer terminal in the luggage check stand: "Sorry sir, number 1702."

"Yes, that's it. 1702. Key's in it." I donned my sunglasses again and swooshed past the confused welcome party and into the lower lobby.

As I entered the elevator I realized that I hadn't eaten since some point the day before. For some reason I didn't feel hungry though.

The doors dinged open on seventeen. It was a suites level, of course. I started to drag a little as I found my way to 1702. I had no idea what I was going to say, but I banged on the door with my right fist before I had a chance to think myself out of it. The door started to open almost immediately.

"Honey please, I can hear you-" Claire Upton sounded pretty chipper. She opened the door wide, resulting in the air being knocked out of both of us.

Mrs. Upton wore only an indecently short nightie of what appeared to be light blue silk. The garment of course echoed her own very sparkly blue eyes. These goddamn Upton women and their eyes... Her dirty blonde hair was down this time, and tumbled around her shoulders. She looked about twenty years younger than the last time I'd seen her in my office. Her new look was probably emphasized by her own long legs, which were just as long as her daughters'. I suppose they had to get it from somewhere, and it wasn't going to be from their golem-esque father.

Having said all this, all the features added up to a very surprised, and increasingly unhappy woman; I was definitely not who she wanted, or expected, to see that morning. She didn't try to close the door in my face though, so I invited myself in and pushed past her.

"Mr. um, whoever you are again, what do you think you're doing?! Get out!" The blue eyes had been replaced with a rotten grey color that reminded me of petrified wood.

I spun back around and the indignation on Mrs. Upton's face was almost hilarious. She stamped over to the phone.

"I just came from your daughter's, the live one." She picked up the receiver and hit the button for the front desk. It made me sweat a little. "Your husband is quite a bastard. And a sexual deviant to boot, no less. You were right, East Coasters are a little different I guess." I kept standing there, and she finally made the move to hang up the phone, slowly. Her eyes lightened a bit, and she ran a hand through her hair. I loosened up a tad, as I was previously bracing to tangle with some security-types when my gambit failed. I guess not *every* morning is terrible.

"Alright, we can talk. Just a moment." No resistance at all. She walked over to the closet and pulled out a fluffy white robe. As she turned away from me to put it on, I recognized a familiar hitch in her step. Focus. She turned back around, walked over to the bed, sat down and crossed her legs, her hands crossed in her lap.

"Did Stacy tell you? About what her father did to them?" She asked like she was about to try to mother me too. All pleasant, no suspicion.

"My investigation was pointing toward such things, she just confirmed it. When did you know?" This is where my observations needed to be completely on the level, but I was starting to run a tad low on energy.

"I'm not sure how much I should reveal to you, Mr.- I'm sorry, I've forgotten your name."

"Marsden."

"Mr. Marsden. I know my daughter hired you, but as she's now passed on, I'm not even sure what you're doing here." She had me there; I could barely comprehend that fact myself. My head swirled a little. I decided to browbeat since I was out of patience, and probably legal footing.

"Mrs. Upton, this is it. Really. When did you know your husband was abusing your daughters? Stacy is still alive, and she needs help." The line I'd drawn between A and B was definitely a little blurred, but I just needed to know.

She stared at me for a good long while. I don't think I gave her much, though I probably looked pretty shabby after the binge of the last twenty four hours.

"Early enough. Too early." It was an answer suitable for an overly dramatic soap opera. But her candor made my skin crawl. I took a step forward and wanted to slap the woman into oblivion. She was showing about as much emotion as an Easter Island rock. Then I got hungry.

I slowly turned around. In front of the picture window, which provided a very romantic view of the Hollywood sign, was a breakfast tray placed on a small table. Two places set. Dishes under chrome plate covers. Smelled like French toast and dark coffee. I lifted one of the covers. Bingo, French toast. I was still competent, and more importantly, perfectly positioned, in my mind.

I swiveled back around and looked at Mrs. Upton. All of a sudden her face regained the years it had seemingly shed when I'd first walked in. She clutched at the lapels of her robe, and I could see her knuckles go white. She appeared to be holding her breath.

I couldn't help but sneer, "Mrs. Upton, I'm terribly sorry, what did I interrupt?" Moments like that only happen a few times in one's life.

She opened her mouth, but no words came out. They were replaced by two sets of playful taps on the door. My eyes darted to the source of the noise, then they came back and I saw her staring at the door too. Me versus a sixty-something? No problem. When I'm fresh of course.

I started toward the door and she played it classic, so classic. She tripped me and I fell flat on my face. As I recovered from being punted by an AARP member, I saw her almost at the door. I lunged forward and caught one of her feet mid stride. She hit the door with her face, which was at least slightly satisfying. But she caught the door handle with her hand and the door swung open as she fell.

The previously missing Mr. Daniel Upton stood there, wide-eyed. He was wearing a dark zip-up hooded sweatshirt meant for someone less than half his age. It looked like he was trying to impersonate a teenager. This was getting a little too strange for my sleep-deprived brain.

He finally registered that I shouldn't have been present in the room his wife was also occupying. I guess I didn't look friendly at that moment, either. He bolted.

"No!" It was more of a moan than a scream from Mrs. Upton. I took the opportunity to silence her with a kick to the stomach as I shoved her out of the way enough for me to slip through the door. Of course Mr. Upton was gone by the time I tripped into the hallway, but I was willing to bet on my knowledge of the hotel versus his. The exit stairway door was just hissing itself closed.

I slammed into one of the elevators and urged it with some button mashing toward the upper lobby level, the terminus of the stairs. I took a moment to review myself in the polished brass of the elevator car. I wasn't a pretty sight. I felt like that's what I should look like at that moment however, so I steeled myself, and as the doors opened, I hurtled out like an Olympic sprinter.

Unfortunately, though my knowledge may have been ahead of the game, the quixotic, antique elevators weren't. I looked right at the most obvious exit point for Mr. Upton, and nothing happened. The fire door didn't open. Then I saw why. Through the glass double doors, I could see Mr. Upton was struggling to hail a cab on Hollywood Boulevard. I couldn't help but emit a very audible sigh as I sprinted for the exit.

I breached the doors just as he tumbled into an orange hybrid taxi. It plunged east down the boulevard almost immediately. It didn't seem fair.

Of course I was immediately blinded by the rising sun as I tried to track the taxi. Goddamn mornings; I'll never give in. But then chance decided to, for once, crack my way. A setup for a premier at the Chinese Theater. There was Upton, stuck in a line of cars a few hundred feet to the east, and he hadn't seen me.

I ran back to the front of the hotel and got them to wrangle my car as fast as the spikey haired moron could manage. I exited and turned onto the boulevard, planting myself into the traffic jam. I wanted to rev my engine, but then realized that would be futile as not only was it an automatic, but we were separated by at least three cars. I couldn't stifle a certain level of endorphins from invading my brain though.

The traffic control boys finally let us through five minutes later. I followed at what would probably be deemed a far too-limited distance, but figured Upton wouldn't be savvy enough to look out for a tail. Then I tried to suppress my adrenaline, which was urging my body to simply get out and mash his face into a pulp.

Upton's taxi went all the way to Gower, up to Franklin, then up Beachwood. It made a turn down one of those very inaccessible, windy streets that have a great city view and zero parking. I tried to hang back, then saw him dash from the car to a house that appeared to be suspended above a canyon–probably on stilts. It'd never make it through a real earthquake event. Wait, that was…good? I needed to get a grip. I had the location, and now I needed to do the rest by the book. Of course, the book.

I did manage to find a space a little farther down the street. I cut the motor, left the keys in the ignition and folded my hands over the wheel. There were a million ways to move forward now, but I wasn't sure which one I wanted-ed to pursue. I could verify Mr. Upton's guilt from both of the sister's testimony, though one of them was dead and the other was questionable in terms of a legal perspective. Mrs. Claire Upton had confirmed it too, but no way she'd open herself up to such liability.

Then I thought of Stacy. There was a certain fear as she described what her father had done to her. Then there was something…else.

The ballerina. Her eyes. I would never leave out her legs. Then her, floating face down in the pool. I was way out of line to think I should pursue the case. Although, it wasn't even really a case anymore. A vendetta would've been the closest definition that made sense, but I decided sometimes vendettas were warranted. Damn, when was the last time I'd slept?

■ ■ ■

It was the most fulfilled I'd felt in about a lifetime. There was the ballerina; she was floating in the pool, naked, of course. I moved over to the edge. I reached out for her, like I'd fantasized just a short time before, but she looked up before I could make a move. Her eyes were the expected beams of opal as they raked me up and down. She slowly and gracefully paddled over. Instead of just floating, she was on a silver, inflatable pool mattress. Her lithe form was pristine. She meandered over toward me in an unnatural way and was about to slide herself onto the pool deck, when I noticed the gigantic slit across her neck. There's no way the remaining flaps of skin would ever support the weight of her head. I dove forward to try to stop her from using her neck, that would kill her for sure. No!

Damn it. I awoke to my head jetting forward toward the windshield. I stopped just short of bashing through it. It was too much. I didn't know whether to trust myself. I decided to hedge my bets.

Ringing. Quinlin picked up on number two, which was pretty exciting.

"Quin, you're going to love this. I broke your case for you." Maybe my gushing made him slightly uncomfortable, maybe it was just early. It definitely was early.

"What? Marsden? What's up? Which case you talking about? Your ballerina?" It was a little unsettling that he thought the ballerina was mine too, but I decided to let it ride.

"I'm outside your murderer's house. For all of them. The ballerina, her husband, all of them." I decided to leave him guessing about Talbot, or at least how much I knew about it.

"Jesus, where are you?" I could hear the engines of justice spooling up in the background. Quinlin would probably be standing by now, and coaxing investigators and cops alike to get their asses in gear. Then he'd wipe his brow, which had begun to sweat fifteen seconds before.

I told him the address, or as close as I could approximate it. I also told him where I'd been earlier.

"Alright, just sit tight Marsden, we're on our way-", I hung up out of habit, and probably because I knew I wasn't going to wait for the cavalry. This was my collar, even though I wasn't a cop. But I *was* mad. I looked in the rearview and again surveyed my destroyed visage. I thought it had improved. Chases always inject energy into a hairstyle. I felt like I was drunk, and maybe I was slightly, from the night before. Just a bit.

Doors unlock, one opens, then closes. I'm outside and ready to go. I look again in the window of my lovely car. I didn't know what would happen, but I knew I should pursue it is far as it could go before Quin got there. Self-examination done, I moved in the direction of Upton's, carelessly.

33

I walked right up to the door, deciding any deception wouldn't be worth my effort. The house was another mid-century deal, with a door that looked original. I raised my hand to knock, then stopped abruptly. This man would be paranoid. I knocked softer than I otherwise would have, then put my ear to the door. Nothing. Something. A slight, cautious padding along carpet. I waited until it stopped, then I stood back and kicked at the handle. The door splintered open almost too easily, whacking Mr. Upton in the face. I myself was immediately hit in the face with a scent I could only define as turpentine mixed with dead roses. He stepped back a few feet, but was able to maintain his balance. He looked nothing like the stoic character from the coffee shop I'd seen days before. Demolished. This was my most bad-ass moment, and only a sexually deviant pedophile was there to witness it. Another one for the resume. I walked in past him and he didn't bother to try to stop me.

"Who are you?" From behind two hands that were holding a bloodied nose.

"My name's Duncan Marsden. You might recognize me from the Roosevelt earlier today. Your daughter hired me to track down your other daughter and figure out why she was having pornographic pictures taken of herself." I decided not to wait for any explanations. "I'm willing to bet you're behind basically all of it, Mr. Upton. You're... such a goddamn asshole." I was now wanting for some energy, as it hit me that I'd let another meal escape.

"I know, I know, but really, I love them." A little unexpected coupled with extremely expected. These types always justified their actions with moronic clichés.

"I'm not even going to argue with you, Mr. Upton. I just want to know the truth, what happened?"

"How do you mean?" I would've gotten dark at that point, but it seemed like he really meant it, which was chilling.

"One of your daughters is dead, her husband is dead. Why did you kill her?" I turned and leveled a stare at him that should've cut him to pieces. Instead, it made his mind explode all over the place.

"I didn't kill them! I didn't kill anyone! I really did love them! I didn't have much choice-." His pathetic logic was starting to grind on my energy-starved brain. I stepped toward him and he started to cower against one of the walls. The man was made of tissue paper. I held a fist over him, which cast a satisfying shadow over his bloodied face.

"I just wanted to see how Marie was doing, I wanted... an update. I approached her very nice husband. He really was sweet. But he said I couldn't. I got upset."

It was like talking to a deranged adolescent.

"He offered to update me on Stacy instead. He said he'd find a way for me to get updates on Stacy if I left Marie alone. That's all I know."

His euphemistic use of "updates" made me gnash my molars.

He sat down and exhaled, as though a massive load had been lifted from his shoulders. I decided to make myself feel a little better. I took aim at his jaw and threw a right hook directly into the center of his skull. My knuckles immediately complained about the decision, but the effect was worth it. His head hit the wall and bounced off, as some blood spattered on the floor next to him. Here was a man who had abused both of his daughters in a way that would forever define their lives. He took pictures of them doing things to each other, and presumably to himself, that were usually only reserved for the most despicable corners of the internet. Of course that meant there was an audience. He was one of them. God damn it. I moved to swing again and he shrunk down even more, anticipating the hit.

He was beyond wretched. I realized that my ballerina's oafish husband had been an accessory to Mr. Upton's contemptible habit. While Costello did legitimately care about

Marie, he was willing to sacrifice Stacy in the process. It became clear to me that Costello had hired Talbot the wannabe pornographer to photograph Stacy. I didn't immediately see how Talbot had gotten to Stacy, but it didn't mean that much at the moment either. I had the man who had twisted the ballerina's life into a tragedy.

I decided to do some real detective work to cover myself. Given his bludgeoned condition, Mr. Upton was going nowhere as he struggled to sit up. I looked around and found a regular living room. Then I saw a brown wood-grain door.

Some more splintering wood, and I'd found the stash. It was a treasure trove of illicit photography. Both sisters in a variety of perverse poses. Of course their father made his way into the pictures as well. Him with her, him with Stacy. Behind. On top. Him with both of them doing things they clearly didn't enjoy. It would've been hard, since neither one could've been more than about fifteen. Their bodies were still silky and unspoiled. Incest was always a taboo, but again, a market exists. My ballerina was tarnished, and she was still perfect.

It would've been so easy to snap his wobbly neck, right there and then. No problem at all. But then, a recognizable sound of tires on pavement. Quinlin must've been pulling up. I cursed of course, but knew I'd probably be saved a murder rap and I was pretty tired after all.

I left the crumpled Mr. Upton against the wall and walked over to the splintered front door, which had managed to close itself. I expected to find a slightly peeved Quinlin on the other side. Boy did I get that wrong.

The door swung inward and revealed a familiar figure. I didn't quite get how familiar immediately. He had one hand on the right side of his stomach. Only a few spots of blood had seeped through his shirt. Must've changed it since I'd shot him in Stacy's apartment earlier that day. Then a whole bunch of billiard balls flooded my slushy brain. Mr. Connecticut PI was standing with an automatic pistol aimed at my face. Why you're always supposed to ask who it is before you open the door, I guess.

"Well, you took your sweet time, huh?" I said it, but he just cracked a shit-eating grin and pulled the hammer back on his gun. "How'd you find us?"

"Just followed. Had to wait till I was sure you wasn't a cop and they weren't with you."

"So Mr. Comor who are you, really?" Might as well maximize my limited time.

"Since it don't matter anymore, it's actually Comare. And I ain't from Connecticut, I'm from Staten Island."

"You didn't strike me as the Connecticut type. You said a broad hired you right?"

"Yeah, the old one." I took that to mean Mrs. Claire Upton.

"You killed the husband, and Marie…the ballerina." He only shook his head "yes" and grinned again. I felt like I could probably handle two shots to the chest if I rushed him. My heart gave me the all-green. Before my mind could make itself up, he motioned for me to move back inside and I instinctually followed his direction.

"I don't know why I's hired to kill em'. I just get paid, you know? It's how this business works. This guy was supposed to be next, but I guess she'll get you for free. " We had both forgotten about Mr. Upton, who was sitting on one of the couches, wide eyed and trying to stem the blood draining from multiple lesions on his face.

"And the panties in the husband's mouth?"

"Just some window dressing, you know, to throw the cops and whatnot." At least he was pretty forthcoming. "You guys were having a fun time yourselves eh?" Mr. Comare chuckled and motioned that I should sit next to Mr. Upton on the couch. I'd be damned.

"Come on Marsden, the jig's up. I gotcha and you just be ok with it, alright?" I decided right then and there he could gun me down anywhere but on the couch sitting next to Mr. Father-of-the-Year. I made to lunge forward, but it turned into more of a self-trip. My forehead hit the very surprised Comare's right shin with a crack, which somehow caused him to lose his grip on his gun. Amateur hour. Before he could go after it, I reached up and punched the gruff Italian right in the balls. He folded in half and I decided to deliver several other blows to his kidneys to make sure he knew who was in charge.

The problem was, it turned out Daniel Upton was now in charge. He had retrieved the hitman's gun and was vacillating between aiming at me or the doubled-over other man. I was about to say something, when I heard yet another car pull up outside, followed by what sounded like a few more.

Daniel didn't pick up on this, as Quinlin punted in the tattered door and aimed his revolver immediately at Mr. Upton. The two officers with him followed suit. Mr. Upton didn't stand a chance, so he did the only thing he was capable of: he shot at Quinlin, or tried to.

A volley directed at Quin. Comare and myself dove for cover. Utilizing unnatural speed, Quin hit the deck, but one of his cohorts managed to get a well-directed shot off before he went down in a spiral of pain.

Mr. Upton didn't hesitate. The shot had hit him in the gun arm, and he'd dropped the piece as he retreated through a back hallway. I looked up just in time to see him disappear into the abyss of another wing of the house.

"Jesus Marsden, I said to wait!" The least of my worries. I took advantage of the lull to kick Mr. Comare one more time. "Quin, here's your murderer, I'm going after Upton."

"You're one lucky son of a gun Marsden. Perfect timing on my part, I will say." I imagined he would take out his handkerchief to blot a job well done. But he simply straightened his coat like a real person as he stood up.

"I don't count just being alive to be all that lucky these days." It was a pithy, dark comment. And I meant every word of it.

34

I picked up Upton's dropped pistol and headed into the abyss myself.

A wheezing "go" from Quinlin is all I heard as I started to attempt to track Daniel Upton through a shitty mid-century at what was rapidly becoming sunset.

I moved through the dimming hallway, gun up and ready to apprehend. It was getting intense, as I edged my way into what appeared to be a bedroom. I looked left and saw the Capital Records building, The Knickerbocker and some other Hollywood landmarks out the sliding glass door. Then I saw a blur in front of them and I fired. I hit the man in the closest leg. I shot two more times to shatter the door and moved to rush him. Before I could, he vaulted over the railing, but realized his mistake in mid-air. His good hand caught one of the cables that formed part of the railing. I ran over and made to grab the bastard and haul him over the rail, to justice, of course.

As I was about to clamp his arm with my other hand, I looked up, and let the scene set in. He was dangling probably about a hundred feet above the next home down the hillside; the house's stilts adding some height to an already precarious position. The monster was about to fall. I could see the blood draining from his fingers; the sweat seeping from every pore on his brow. He looked up. He had dead eyes; they were trembling.

The ballerina invaded my perception. It wasn't even her nudity this time. It was her visage from our last drink together. There was hope, there was seduction, there was just too much to destroy for some shitty reason... I only wanted her, only her.

I grabbed Daniel Upton's other hand when he desperately grasped upward. He awaited his catapult into the custody of the LAPD. Then my mind snapped to a television show I'd seen a week or so before.

The fictional D.A. had made a big point about the law being separate from justice. Sometimes the law perverts justice for the good of society, he insisted. You have to trust society in the end.

Without so much as a flinch, as soon as I was sure I was his only anchor, I let go. I desperately wanted to see him torn up on the roof of the house below, but as the sun had already set, I had to settle for a resounding thud that echoed through the canyon.

My mind immediately recoiled from my action. I'd just broken the law. Then I reminded myself, the whole reason for laws was to deliver justice. I'd delivered justice. Sometimes a jury doesn't need to be poisoned by a morally reprehensible individual. Maybe society needed some help sometimes.

Before my rationalizations could escalate to another level, a hand was on my shoulder, and made to pull me around. My first reaction was to resist.

Quin was standing there. He had a textbook blank look.

"Jumped huh?"

"Yeah he fell, hit a house sounded like."

"Well, let's go collect the pieces, eh?"

35

Daniel Upton was right where I'd left him. He'd hit the chimney of the house below, which had broken his back and killed him. Quin had called for high-powered lights to be brought in so the crime scene could be processed that night. No need to draw it out, he said.

Upton had lived a few moments after hitting the chimney the M.E. explained. I felt the hair on my neck stand up. Justice only took one broken back, and it wasn't even mine.

I pulled Quin out of the crowd and toward a cascade of bougainvillea along the hillside. "So, what about the wife? Mrs. Upton?"

"I sent some unis down to pen her in right after your call. She should still be there, unless she decided to off herself, which would be pretty dramatic." He was trying to add some levity to a bad situation. I appreciated that.

"Daniel Upton didn't kill anyone. The ballerina, her husband- I have an idea who might've, but I suppose we should get her side, if we can." Quinlin only nodded in agreement and clapped me on the back.

He said his goodbyes, grabbed a driver and headed down the hill toward Hollywood in a cruiser. As he had to stop at the Hollywood substation briefly to make some sort of report, I had time to return my car to my place before any big revelations were spouted.

I walked back to my own car, unlocked her and got inside. I took a deep breath, smelled the leather. Then I started weaving my own way out of the hills and back into Hollywood proper. Apparently in the scuffle I'd cut a knuckle and bruised one of my knees. As I rubbed them therapeutically, I slowly worked my way back down Hollywood Boulevard toward my complex.

After hurriedly parking, I legged it toward The Roosevelt immediately. On the way over I saw couples, singles, seedy groups, all enjoying themselves, looked like. People could still experience joy. Neat.

Then I spied Quinlin with his driver motoring by, and I bummed a ride for the last five hundred feet in the barred back seat. Always good to make an entrance. We pulled up a few moments later, no sirens, and the valet looked pretty spooked as Quinlin motioned to have my rear, barred door opened. He timidly obliged. I thought that was pretty funny, given my dealings with Daniel Upton the night before; the poor valet had unwittingly freed a murderer. No wait—a judge.

Seventeen dinged in the elevator, and we all got out. We proceeded to the only door with two uniformed cops outside it. Without a word, they saw Quin and unlocked the door.

Mrs. Claire Upton was sitting at the desk, adjusting her makeup in the reflection of the window that looked out over Hollywood. Her hair was up; the matron was back.

Quinlin started: "Mrs. Upton, you're under—"

"Mr. Quin-something, is it?" She couldn't have been haughtier. I waited for her to offer us a piece of cake.

"I'm not sure you understand who I am, but I'm Mrs. Claire Upton of *The* Uptons." Quinlin was about to interrupt again to finish Mirandizing her, but she wouldn't hear of it. "You, this private detective he said he was, this whole city. None of you understand the ramifications of what's going on right here, right now. You've come to arrest me no doubt, and you're in the wrong. You can't build a society without families like ours. We've been the bedrock of America for a hundred years. You need *good* people to keep society ripe and flourishing. We are good people." She looked at me, and took a small step toward me. "Do you realize how hard it is to find good people Mr. Marsden? Good, meritorious people?"

She looked down on us as though we were grade school students in for detention. Even so, there was a tinge of desperation in her interrogative. She kept going: "The problem with the world today is simply too many people. There are simply too many, and too many who aren't kept in check. Society needs a release valve. That's what I've provided." She stopped and looked around expectantly. No one could believe this was her real defense, but her eyes said it absolutely was.

"I may have dealt with my family in my own way, but it was for the good of society. I know that's more of a novel concept in this particular state, but back home I'm sure they'd understand. My husband was corrosive, and my daughter was an unfortunate casualty. But she didn't die without *just* cause. There's no way the Upton name was going to be stained with the contemptible actions of these men I dealt with, nor by the exposure generated by my daughter's investigation. We represent a symbol of American moral certainty. When I found out my husband's habit had reemerged, I was left with few options."

"We are lacking a great number of morally righteous people in today's world. When my family came to prominence, we were in the company of the Rockefellers, the Roosevelts. Families that understood the meaning of a meritocracy and how important a leading class of people above reproach was to this nation. They would've understood that it was my duty not only to shield the public from my family's indiscretions, but make sure they wouldn't contaminate our own societal class. Look at who's running our country now. We need this kind of justice to ensure that progress can continue!"

I looked around and saw only frozen faces. Everyone obviously thought this woman's diatribe was insane. The last bit was especially over the top, but I tried to think through her points anyway and found that, had I been sitting behind my scuffed desk in my stuffy office watching a live stream, I might've agreed with what she'd done and toasted the outcome. Then my mind came to a screaming halt, when I remembered Mrs. Upton had tried to kill Stacy and myself as well. And that my ballerina was dead.

As if on cue, Quinlin walked up and put a finger to her lips. He finished Mirandizing her and handcuffed her, which obviously confused her very much. The lady was crazy, and maybe she was right, and just doing what every family should do when there's a cancerous tumor in their midst. I just didn't see how the ballerina fit that description. Then I remembered I *still* hadn't eaten, and quieted my mind.

Quinlin led her out amidst her protests. I saw that her room had a mini bar, which contained mini bottles of bourbon. I helped myself to a miniature drink, felt a little better, then regretted it.

Downstairs, the media had already gathered, as there was a high profile arrest going on at the Roosevelt Hotel, after all. A local reporter asked who the suspect was; Quinlin simply said Mrs. Claire Upton, of Connecticut. The reporter scratched his chin, then turned back to his producer to discuss what he should actually tell the people of Los Angeles.

I followed the media circus outside, and watched Mrs. Upton get loaded into the back of a cruiser. Quinlin then went shotgun again and tipped an imaginary hat to me. I managed a smile, a very tired smile.

36

I opted to walk back to my apartment in the morning light. On the plus side, I'd at least had a very productive night. The new sunlight couldn't dilute that fact. As I stepped off the curb at Hollywood and Highland, I tried to parse the fact that life was essentially a series of ledges. The trick is jumping, and not falling. I snickered a bit given what I'd witnessed the night before, and picked up my pace. My bed was calling to me.

Unlock, elevator up, unlock again. Inside. Finally. There was nothing left to think about. It was almost 10 a.m. and I hadn't slept since…the last time I was asleep. I collapsed into bed. No more than fifteen minutes later, a notification on my phone roused me. I wanted to sigh, but saw it was Stacy. All she said was: "Saw what happened on the news. I want to talk to you in person." The only thing that stuck with me was that she didn't say "thank in person." I would've worried, if I could stay awake.

I'd drifted off again when I was awoken by a knock at my door. First I grasped for my gun, then I remembered it was probably Stacy and decided to throw caution to the wind. I dragged myself off my bed, through the living room and finally to the door. I opened and she came wafting in. She was wearing a miniskirt, a white blouse and some demure high heels, if such a thing exists.

"I just wanted to come by to thank you personally." She was being as grown up as possible. And she even smiled.

"Thank me for what?"

"Well, my father's dead, and my mother's in prison, isn't that right?" She walked over, sat down on my couch and crossed her legs.

"He is dead, and your mother is under arrest in fact, though you're right, she'll probably end up in prison. In California of all places. Just her luck." I smiled and she, for once, smiled right back. It was remarkable, as I couldn't recall seeing her smile ever before. I was about to ask her why she had gotten involved with Talbot's pornography angle, then realized for her that probably wasn't an angle at all. Quinlin had said that the envelopes found in her apartment had been repurposed. She'd probably been approached by Talbot innocently enough. She'd been paid for her work. Probably some cash sourced directly from her father, since it was his address that had been crossed out on the envelopes. I decided it was a can of worms nobody needed.

I evaluated her outfit again. It was provocative, but classy. Exactly like her sister. I was running on fumes and decided to call it.

"Well, you're welcome I guess. I'm sorry about your sister. Your parents were...well there's no other way to put it, they were terrible, Stacy." I pulled out a chair from my small dining table and took a seat opposite her. She realized I wasn't going to say anything else.

"Mr. Marsden, I hope I never see you again." She accompanied it with the same smile as before, but this time it stung a little.

Stacy got up. I got up. She came over and hugged me, reverently, if I'm truthful. There was going to be no carnal payoff with this one, and that was probably fine.

She left without looking back. I took a seat again in the chair I'd pulled out, and looked out the window at Hollywood Boulevard, past my lone palm tree. The tree swayed just a tad.

I tried to reflect on everything that had transpired over the last week: Three murders, a fourth death, and a tired Marsden. Nothing had changed. But nothing would ever change, not the way I had things going, because people are stupid and always try to get away with the same shit. I just had to avoid stepping in it.

Made in the USA
San Bernardino, CA
10 November 2019